THE CASE OF THE
Stepdaughter's Secret

Erle Stanley Gardner

THE CASE OF THE

Stepdaughter's Secret

WALTER J. BLACK · ROSLYN, N. Y.

THE CASE OF THE
Stepdaughter's Secret

At approximately ten-forty-five, Della Street nervously began looking at her wrist watch.

Perry Mason interrupted his dictation to smile at her.

"Della, you're nervous as a cat."

"I can't help it," she said. "To think that Mr. Bancroft telephoned for the earliest possible appointment—and the way his voice sounded over the telephone!"

"And you told him that he could have an eleven o'clock appointment if he could get here at that time," Mason said.

She nodded. "He said that he'd have to stretch the speed limit to get here, but he'd make it if it was humanly possible."

"Then," Mason said, "Harlow Bissinger Bancroft will be here at eleven o'clock. His time is valuable. Every minute is metered, and he plans his business along those lines."

"But what could he possibly want with an attorney who specializes in the defense of criminal cases?" Della asked. "Good heavens, the legal secretaries say that he has more corporations than a dog has fleas. He has a battery of attorneys who do nothing but handle his work. I understand there are seven lawyers alone in the tax division."

Mason glanced at his watch. "Wait eleven minutes and you'll find out. Somehow, I—"

The ringing of the telephone interrupted him.

Della Street picked up the telephone, said to the receptionist, "Yes, Gertie. . . . Just a moment," placed her hand over the mouthpiece, said to Mason, "Mr. Bancroft is in the office, saying he managed to get here a little early, that he'll wait until eleven if he can't see you before, but that the time element is highly important."

Mason said, "Evidently it's more of an emergency than I thought. Bring him in, Della."

Della Street folded her shorthand book with alacrity, jumped to her feet and hurried into the outer office. A few moments later she was back with a man in his middle fifties, a man whose close-cropped gray mustache emphasized the determination of his mouth. He had steel-gray eyes and a manner of crisp authority.

"Mr. Bancroft," Mason said, rising and extending his hand.

"Mr. Mason," Bancroft said. "Good morning—and thank you for seeing me so promptly."

He turned and glanced at Della Street.

"Della Street, my confidential secretary," Mason explained. "I like to have her sit in on all of my interviews and make notes."

"This is highly confidential," Bancroft said.

"And she is highly competent and accustomed to keeping confidences inviolate," Mason said. "She knows everything about all of my cases."

Bancroft sat down. Suddenly, the air of decision and self-assertion vanished. The man seemed to melt down inside his clothes.

"Mr. Mason," he said, "I'm at the end of my rope. Everything that I have worked for in my life, everything I have built up, is tumbling down like a house of cards."

"Come, now, it can't be *that* serious," Mason told him.

"It is."

"Suppose you tell me just what's bothering you," Mason said, "and we'll see what we can do about it."

Almost pathetically, Bancroft extended his two hands. "Do you see these?" he asked.

Mason nodded.

"I have built everything in life with these two hands," Bancroft said. "They have been my means of support. I have worked as a day laborer. I have fought and struggled to get ahead. I have gone into debt until I felt there was no possible way of paying off the indebtedness and achieving financial stability. I have sat tight when it seemed that my whole empire was about to come crashing down. I have fought through adverse conditions and faced enemies with not a single ace in the hole but an ability to bluff them into submission. I have gambled by staking my fortune to buy when everyone else was in a panic to sell, and now these hands hold my undoing."

"Why?" Mason asked.

"Because of the fingertips," Bancroft said.

"Go on," Mason told him, his eyes narrowing.

"I am a so-called self-made man," Bancroft said. "I ran away from home when there wasn't much of a home to keep me. I got tangled up with some rather wild associates, I learned a lot of things that I shouldn't have known. I learned how to short-cut the ignition wiring on cars, I learned how to make a living in dark alleys, so to speak, by stealing hubcaps, spare tires and automobiles.

"I was finally caught and sent to the penitentiary, which probably was the best thing that ever happened to me.

"When I went to the penitentiary, I had a resentment against society. I thought that I had been caught simply because I had been imprudent and I resolved to be more cunning when I got out and to continue my nefarious work so that I wouldn't be caught again.

"There was a chaplain in that prison who took an interest in me. I won't say that he gave me religion, because, in a way, he didn't. He simply gave me confidence in myself and my fellow man, and in a divine scheme of the universe.

"He pointed out that life was too complicated to be accidental, that it took a master plan to account for life, as we knew it; that fledglings emerged from the egg, grew feathers and poised on the edge of the nest with the desire to fly because of what we call instinct; that instinct was merely a divine plan and a means by which the architect of that divine plan communicated with the living units.

"He asked me to consult my own instincts, not my selfish inclinations but the feelings that came to me when I could deliberately disregard my environment and put myself in harmony with the universe. He dared me to surrender myself in the solitude of night to the great heart of the universe."

"And you did?" Mason asked.

"I did it because he told me I was *afraid* to do it, and I wanted to show him I wasn't. I wanted to prove he was wrong."

"And he wasn't wrong?"

"Something came to me—I don't know what it was. A feeling of awareness, a desire to make something of myself. I started to read, study and think."

Mason regarded him curiously. "You have traveled considerably, Mr. Bancroft. What do you do about passports?"

"Fortunately," Bancroft said, "I started out with enough family pride to conceal my real name. The one I used in the penitentiary, the name that I used during all of the period of wildness, was not the name with which I had been christened. I managed to preserve my incognito."

"But your fingerprints?" Mason asked.

"There's the rub," Bancroft said. "If my fingerprints are ever taken and sent to the F.B.I., within a matter of minutes it will become known that Harlow Bissinger Bancroft, the great philanthropist and financier, is a criminal who served fourteen months in a penitentiary."

"All right," Mason said. "Quite evidently, someone has discovered the secret of your past."

Bancroft nodded.

"And threatens to expose it?" Mason asked. "Are you being asked to pay blackmail?"

By way of answer, Bancroft took a sheet of paper from his pocket and handed it to Mason.

The paper had a typewritten message:

Get fifteen hundred dollars in ten and twenty dollar bills. Put them in a red coffee can, together with ten silver dollars. Put the lid on tight and await telephone instructions as to the time and place of disposal. Put this note in with the money so we'll know the police won't try to trace us through the typing. If you follow instructions to the letter, you have nothing to fear, otherwise the family will face the disgrace of knowing whose fingerprints are on file and where.

Mason studied the paper carefully. "And this was sent to you through the mail?"

"Not to me," Bancroft said, "but to my stepdaughter, Rosena Andrews."

Mason raised inquiring eyebrows.

"Seven years ago I married," Bancroft said. "My wife was a widow. She had a daughter, Rosena, who was then sixteen. She is now twenty-three. A very beautiful, intense young woman, who is engaged to be married to Jetson Blair of the socially prominent Blair family."

Mason's eyes became thoughtful. "Why would they strike at her instead of at you?"

"Because," Bancroft said, "they wanted to emphasize the fact that she was the more vulnerable, particularly during this period of her engagement."

"A wedding date has been set?" Mason asked.

"It has not been formally announced, but they expect to be married in about three months."

"And how did you get this?" Mason asked.

"I knew that my stepdaughter was tremendously upset over something. She came in the door with an envelope in her hand and her face was as white as a sheet. She had planned to go swimming in the afternoon, but rang up Jetson Blair and canceled the date, saying she wasn't feeling well.

"I knew something was wrong.

"Rosena made an excuse to leave and go to the city. I assumed she wanted to see her mother, who was spending the night in our apartment here in the city. She left early this morning. Well, Mr. Mason, after she had left I went to her room. I found this letter under the blotter of her desk."

"Now, let's get this straight," Mason said. "You say she came to the city and you assumed she wanted to see her mother."

"Her mother is in the city, making arrangements for a charity ball. She spent yesterday and last night in our apartment here. I have been staying with Rosena out at the lake. Rosena's mother is due back at the lake tonight. That's why I wanted to see you at the earliest possible moment. I want to get back to the lake and put this letter where I found it, before Rosena returns."

"Did you tell your wife anything about your criminal record?" Mason asked.

"Heaven help me," Bancroft said, "I did not. I should have. I have cursed myself a thousand times for being too cowardly to do so, but I was very much in love. I knew that, regardless of how much Phyllis loved me, she would never jeopardize the social career of her daughter by marrying a man with a criminal record.

"Now, Mr. Mason, you know my secret. You are the only living person who does."

"Other than the person or persons who sent this letter," Mason said.

Bancroft nodded.

"Rosena has enough money to fulfill these demands?" Mason asked.

"Certainly," Bancroft said. "She has an account of several thousand dollars in her own name, and, of course, she can always get any amount of money from me whenever she asks for it."

"You don't know whether she intends to ignore this demand or to comply with it."

"I feel certain she intends to comply with it."

"That, of course," Mason said, "will be only the first bite. One never finishes with a blackmailer."

"I know, I know," Bancroft said. "But, after all, after three months —that is, after the wedding is over, there won't be so much pressure."

"Not on her," Mason said. "The pressure will then shift to you. You don't think your stepdaughter knows?"

"Evidently she does," Bancroft said. "The people who sent this letter must have telephoned her, giving her enough information so she understands what it is she is trying to avoid. I would certainly assume that to be the case."

"You say you are staying at the lake?"

"At Lake Merticito," Bancroft said. "We have a summer home there."

"I understand," Mason said, "that the lake is highly exclusive, properties run several hundred dollars a front foot."

"That is true," Bancroft said, "except for a three-hundred-foot frontage at the southern end of the lake. That is a public beach and occasionally the characters who come there make trouble. There is a launching ramp, a marina where boats can be rented, and— Well, for the most part, the people who come there are orderly. There is, nevertheless, a certain element of undesirables. They occasionally get out in the lake and make trouble for the regular residents.

"Private property, of course, goes to the edge of the lake at low water and we're able to keep trespassers off the lands that are privately owned. But the lake is ideal for water-skiing, and occasionally some unpleasantness results from this outside element."

"I take it that it is state owned as a park." Mason said.

"No, it is privately owned."

"Why don't the owners get together and buy that strip out?" Mason asked.

"Because of a peculiar provision in the title," Bancroft said. "The property was left to heirs, in trust, with the understanding that for a period of ten years it would be open to the public on charges to be fixed by a board of trustees.

"The owner of the property was a public-spirited citizen who felt that too much waterfront property was being grabbed up by persons of wealth and the public was being excluded."

"How is the property operated?" Mason asked.

"On a very high-class level, so far. The owners have done all they could to exclude the rowdy element. It is, however, open to the public with all that this means."

Mason nodded toward the telephone. "You know where your step-daughter banks," he said. "She has come to town. It is now after eleven o'clock. Ring up her bank and ask for the person in charge of her account. Say that you want to see that nothing is said about it, but identify yourself and ask them if your daughter has made a with-drawal this morning of fifteen hundred dollars in tens and twenties."

Bancroft hesitated a moment, then took the phone that Della Street extended to him, called the manager of the bank, identified himself, said, "I want some highly confidential information. I want nothing to be said about the fact that I have called and I want nothing to be done about it. But I would like to know if my step-daughter has cashed a check this morning on her account. . . . Yes, I'll hold the phone."

Bancroft held the phone for some two minutes, then said, "Hello . . . Yes . . . I see . . . Thank you very much . . . No, say noth-ing about it. . . . No, don't let anyone know that I have called, and forget the whole thing."

Bancroft hung up, turned to Mason and nodded. "She cashed a fifteen-hundred-dollar check," he said, "specifying that the money was to be in ten- and twenty-dollar bills. She also asked for ten sil-ver dollars."

Mason thought for a moment, then said, "I'm going to give you some advice, Bancroft. You probably won't want to follow it."

"What is it?"

"This chaplain who helped straighten you out," Mason asked, "is he still alive?"

"Yes. He now has a rather large church."

"Make a substantial donation to that church," Mason said. "At the time you make the donation, state publicly that you are indebted to him, explain that you are a self-made man, that your past contains some mistakes made in your early youth. In other words, beat them to the punch, stand up on your own two feet and be proud of your record."

Bancroft paled and shook his head. "I simply couldn't do that, Mr. Mason. It would kill my wife. Coming at this time, it would simply kill her. It would put Rosena in an absolutely impossible position."

"Then," Mason said, "prepare to pay and pay and pay."

Bancroft nodded. "I had anticipated that."

"Unless," Mason said, "you are willing to let me have a free hand in the matter."

"I'm perfectly willing to give you a free hand," Bancroft said. "That's why I'm here."

"Sometimes," Mason said, "blackmailers are vulnerable. They can be jailed upon another charge—and, of course, if you appeal to the police, you will find they're most co-operative and—"

"No, no, no," Bancroft said. "We cannot appeal to the police. We cannot let them know. . . . This is too much of a juicy scandal item coming right at this time."

"All right," Mason said, "what I'm going to do is going to cost you some money. It's going to be daring, ingenious, and I hope it will be clever enough to fool the blackmailers."

"What do you mean? What do you have in mind?" Bancroft asked.

Mason said, "Look at this letter carefully. The money is to be put in a large coffee can and the lid put on tight. Ten silver dollars are to be put in the can. Now, what does all this mean?"

"That's what I don't get," Bancroft said.

"It means one thing to me," Mason said. "The blackmailers don't want to show their hand. They don't want to disclose their identity. It means that the can is going to be put in the water and left floating, and then the blackmailers can pick it up. The ten silver dollars will be ballast to keep the can right side up."

"Yes, that's a logical assumption," Bancroft said after thinking for a moment.

"You are living at the lake. I take it your stepdaughter does a lot of water-skiing and swimming."

Bancroft nodded.

"All right," Mason said, "we're going to take a chance. I'm going to have an expert detective shadow your stepdaughter with binoculars. Whenever this can is dropped in the water, I am going to have someone, who will apparently be boating in the lake or fishing, pick up the can, open it, and turn the whole business over to the police."

"What!" Bancroft said, jumping to his feet. "Why, that's exactly the thing that I can't afford. That's—"

"Just a minute," Mason said. "Look the situation over carefully. There is nothing in the letter indicating to whom it was sent. If the person who finds the can with the money in it can pretend to be an innocent fisherman who has found the money and the note and turned it over to the police, the police will publicize the whole thing, the blackmailers will go into a panic and try to figure out some way of beginning all over again. They will be on the defensive and yet they can't claim that they have been betrayed by their victim. They will simply feel the cards went against them. The money will be safe in the hands of the police. The blackmailers will be running for cover."

"They'll strike back," Bancroft said. "They'll publicize the information about me—"

"And kill the goose that's going to lay all their golden eggs?" Mason interposed. "Not a chance."

Bancroft thought the matter over. "It's taking a chance," he said.

"You can't live without taking chances," Mason told him. "If you want a lawyer who *doesn't* take chances, get someone else. This is a calculated risk. It's a good gamble."

Bancroft sighed. "All right. The thing is in your hands."

"Now then," Mason went on, "I'm going to do one more thing, with your permission."

"What?"

"From the wording of the note it would seem there is more than one blackmailer. I'm going to break up the combination if possible."

"How?" Bancroft said.

"It's a scheme I'm turning over in my mind. I'll have to give it further thought," Mason said. "The trouble with a blackmailer is that he always has you on the defensive. *He* calls the turns. *He* tells *you* what to do, how much *he* wants, *where* you make the payment, *when* you make the payment, *how* you make the payment. You resent it and you sputter. But, in the long run, you give in."

Bancroft nodded.

"There are just four ways to deal with a blackmailer," Mason said, holding up his fingers and counting off the points as he made them.

"First, you pay the blackmailer off, thinking that will get him off your neck. That is like chasing a mirage in the desert. A blackmailer never quits.

"Second, you go to the police. You make a clean breast to the police and you lay a trap for the blackmailer and put him in prison, and the police protect your confidence."

Bancroft shook his head decisively.

"Third," Mason said, "you get the blackmailer on the defensive, so that he isn't in a position to call the shots and tell you what to do and when to do it and how to do it. You get him worried. Now, if I'm going to handle this case and I can't go to the police, I'm going to try the third way."

"Isn't that dangerous?" Bancroft asked.

"Sure, it's dangerous," Mason admitted. "But you don't get anywhere in a deal of this kind unless you're willing to take chances."

"What's the fourth way?" Bancroft asked.

"The fourth way," Mason said, smiling wryly, "is to kill the blackmailer—and that has been done from time to time—sometimes with very satisfactory results—though I hardly recommend it."

Bancroft thought for a moment, then said, "It's in your hands. You'll have to try it the third way. But at the start we'll pay off. That will give us a little time."

"That's all you gain by paying off," Mason said, "time."

"How much money do you want?" Bancroft asked.

"Right at the start," Mason said, "I want ten thousand dollars. I'm going to hire the Paul Drake Detective Agency, I'm going to put out a lot of operatives, I'm going to try to find out who these blackmailers are, and when I find out I'm going to keep them so busy with problems of their own that they won't have any time to be putting you and your daughter on the defensive."

"That sounds wonderful," Bancroft said, "*if* you can do it."

"I know," Mason said, "that's a pretty big if. But that's the only way I'll handle it, unless you let me go to the police and tell them the whole story."

Bancroft vehemently shook his head. "I'm too prominent. It would leak out," he said.

"Let it leak," Mason told him. "Proclaim it from the housetops. Go out and stand on your record. Show that rehabilitation is possible."

"Not now, not now," Bancroft said. "The results to my stepdaughter would be disastrous. My wife would never forgive me as long as she lived."

Bancroft took out a checkbook and wrote a check for ten thousand dollars.

"I take it," he said, "this is by way of retainer."

"And to cover initial expenses," Mason told him.

Mason opened a desk drawer, took out a small camera, screwed an extension barrel on the lens, put the blackmail letter down on the desk, mounted the camera on a tripod, took three exposures, said, "That should be enough."

He folded the note and handed it back to Bancroft.

Bancroft said, "You'll never know how much of a load you've taken off my shoulders, Mason."

"It isn't off yet," Mason told him. "And before I get done, you'll probably be cursing me."

"Never," Bancroft said. "I know too much about you, about your reputation for success. Your methods are daring and unconventional, but they pay off."

"I'll do my best," Mason said, "but that's all I can promise. Now, you're going to put this note right back where your stepdaughter can find it when she returns with the money."

"That's right," Bancroft said.

"And then what?"

"Then I'm going to leave things entirely up to you."

"All right," Mason said. "We'll try making an end run, and then see if we can't reverse the field."

2

Paul Drake studied the copy of the blackmail note which Della Street had made on her typewriter.

"What do you make of it?" Mason asked.

"To whom was it sent?"

"To Rosena Andrews, who is the stepdaughter of Harlow Bissinger Bancroft."

Drake whistled.

"Now then," Mason said, "take another look at it. What do you make of it?"

"It's the first bite," Drake said. "If they fall for this, there will be another and another and another."

Mason said, "I know. But look at the note again, Paul. Notice the business about the tightly sealed coffee can, and it has to be a red coffee can, capable of holding the money and ten silver dollars."

"So?" Drake asked.

"So," Mason said, "it means that the delivery is to be made by tossing the can in the water somewhere. And that, after all, is about the best way a blackmailer could work.

"The Bancrofts are at present living at their summer home out on Lake Merticito. Rosena Andrews, the stepdaughter, is an avid water skier.

"My best guess is that the telephoned instructions will be for her to start out water-skiing with the can under her arm, to drop it at a certain spot in the lake, after making certain no other boats are around."

"Then what?" Drake asked.

"Then the blackmailers' boat will swoop out after Rosena is out of sight. They will pick up the coffee can, take out the money and the note, dump the can back in the water, with the lid off so it will sink, and the blackmailers will be merrily on their way."

14

"And so?" Drake asked.

"So," Mason said, "you're going to have to work fast. I want you to round up some female operatives who will look good in bathing suits. If possible, get a starlet who would like to have some publicity in the newspapers. Dress the girls in the briefest bathing suits the law allows, and rent yourself the speediest boat you can find. Get one with twin motors that are souped up so the boat will be capable of having a burst of speed. Get a pair of powerful binoculars and get started."

"What do I do?"

"Go out there and have the girls just act crazy," Mason said. "Have them jumping in the water, flopping around, having water fights, taking sunbaths. Run the boat at trolling speed, and if there is any fishing in the lake, you can have some fishing lines out. Then once in a while give the boat a burst of speed. All the time you'll be hanging around the shoreline where you can keep a watch on the Bancroft residence.

"Sometime this afternoon or tomorrow, you'll see Rosena Andrews coming out on water skis and—"

"How will I recognize her?" Drake asked.

"If she's your pigeon," Mason said, "she'll have a red coffee can under her arm, and the boat will leave from Bancroft's summer home on the lake."

"I see," Drake said.

"She'll go water-skiing or else just be running the boat," Mason said. "You're to make no effort to follow her. You'll be loafing along the shoreline. You watch until she drops the red coffee can. When she drops that coffee can, your girls go crazy. You start the boat out at high speed—not directly for the coffee can, but to try and catch the waves made by the wake of Rosena's boat. You splash up in the waves and have a great time, and then apparently by accident, you pick up this coffee can.

"Now, this is the tricky part of it, Paul. I want you to have a dupli-cate red coffee can. It will, of course, be empty. I want you to go past the can that Rosena drops so you can scoop it up with a landing net, but at exactly that moment, you drop the decoy coffee can into the water and keep right on going, so if anyone should be watching you, the action will be so fast that it will look as if you've simply cut in close to the floating coffee can but haven't paid any particular attention to it."

"That'll take some doing," Drake said.

"That'll take perfect co-ordination, but it can be done," Mason told him.

"You'll be cutting figure eights and circles and you'll have the surface of the lake all churned up with big waves. Have the girls water-skiing if they're expert enough. That can will be up at the top of a wave, then down at the bottom. Anyone watching can't be sure exactly *what* happens. I want you to have at least three, and preferably four, scantily clad girls in the boat. One of them can be a startlet who would like publicity. The others can be female operatives whose discretion you can trust."

"And what do I do with the real coffee can when I get it?"

"You telephone me," Mason said.

"And where will you be?"

"Della and I will be sitting on the porch of the country house of Melton Varas Elliott, that's one of the mansions on the lake. Elliott has had me do work for him and will be glad to accommodate me in a matter of this sort. Once you get that coffee can in your possession, pop it into a bait box of some sort or a canvas duffel bag, so that anyone who is watching won't see what you have.

"And after you've tossed out the decoy and have the real coffee can in your possession, get back to shore someplace where you can keep your eyes on that decoy coffee can. Some boat will come along to pick it up. I want to get the license number of the boat, a description of the people who are in it, and I want to know where they go —but I don't want them to know that they're being followed. That's where your girls are going to have to come in. They'll be cutting all sorts of capers and you apparently will have your attention riveted exclusively on the girls."

"Okay," Drake said, "I'll do my best."

"Get started," Mason told him. "Grab your car, get the girls and head for the lake. You don't have much time. The probabilities are the delivery will take place sometime this afternoon."

"On my way," Drake said, leaving the office.

Mason turned to Della. "Ring up Melton Elliott, Della, and tell him that we want to use his house at Lake Merticito for the afternoon.

"In the meantime, Della, take this roll of film, or have Gertie take this roll of film over to Frank Stenter Dalton, the handwriting expert. Tell him to develop the pictures, make an enlarged print of the blackmail note, determine what make and model of typewriter was used in typing it, and then tell him to buy me a somewhat battered model of the same typewriter.

"Then get me three thousand dollars in tens and twenties," he said, reaching for a checkbook; then added, as something of an afterthought, "you'd better take along a bathing suit, Della. It's a hot day and you might like a swim."

3

The palatial residence of Melton Varas Elliott was across the lake from Harlow Bancroft's home and some distance to the south.

Mason and Della Street sat in the cool shade of the porch, the lawyer holding binoculars to his eyes.

At this hour of the afternoon on a weekday, there was little activity on the lake. Here and there a speedboat, carrying a graceful water skier, cut smooth circles or long, graceful figure S curves. A gentle northerly breeze stirred small wavelets which interfered with the reflections.

A butler, who had been instructed over the telephone by Melton Elliott to see that his guests were given every comfort, brought them cooling drinks and hovered solicitously in the background.

Della, gazing toward the south, said, "I wonder if this is Paul Drake's outfit."

Mason turned the binoculars. Slowly a smile softened his features and he handed the binoculars to Della Street.

"Take a look," he invited.

Della Street held the binoculars to her eyes.

"Good heavens!" she exclaimed, then passed the binoculars back to Mason. "I think you'll enjoy the scenery more than I will," she added dryly.

Mason watched the graceful lines of the speedboat and those of the three feminine figures within it. They were attired in the briefest of bathing suits.

"Looks like Paul Drake at the helm," he said, "well disguised with dark goggles."

"And," Della Street observed, "*he's* getting paid for this—a generous salary and all expenses."

"No doubt about it," Mason said, "I took up the wrong profession."

Drake's boat turned in a burst of speed, came charging up the lake, swept past the Elliott house, then made a sharp turn.

The scantily clad young women screamed. Two of them clung to Drake for support.

"Is he grinning?" Della Street asked.

"I can't even see his face," Mason said, "there are too many girls."

Drake abruptly slowed the boat to a trolling speed.

One of the young women produced water skis, and Drake stopped the boat as she eased herself into the water, then, getting in the proper position, gave a signal.

Drake gunned the boat into speed and the young woman, gracefully coming to the surface of the water on the skis, executed a series of circling maneuvers in back of the boat, crossing and recrossing the waves made by the wake.

"Don't get so wrapped up in Paul Drake," Della Street warned, "that you forget to look at the Bancroft residence. I think a boat just put out from there."

Mason shifted the binoculars.

"It did, for a fact," he said. "A boat with just one person in it. I had rather anticipated there'd be a water skier."

"Regulations provide for two people in the boat when a person is skiing," Della Street said. "One person at the wheel and one person to watch the skier. Perhaps Rosena wants to handle this all by herself."

Mason, studying the lake, said thoughtfully, "There's a fisherman out there, apparently pole fishing with an anchor. There are some boats down nearer the south end of the lake, but no one else is around the Bancroft boat."

"Can you see if she has a red can?" Della Street asked.

Mason shook his head.

Drake's boat picked up speed and made a series of circles.

"Wait a minute," Mason said. "I think she's throwing something overboard. I got a glimpse of something going over, and—it looks as though there might be something red there . . . I can't get a good look at it. There are too many waves, what with the wake of the boat and the waves generated by the wind."

Abruptly, Drake's boat shot into speed.

"Evidently Drake has seen it," Mason said.

The water skier was following in a straight line now, directly behind the boat, as Drake gunned the boat into power, rapidly shorten-
ing the distance to the boat which had put out from the Bancroft
landing.

"Well," Mason said, "he's up to where he should be able to see
the red coffee can if— Oh-oh, there's an accident."

The young woman who was water-skiing behind Drake's boat
tried to make a turn, evidently misjudged a wave and made a som-
ersault into the water.

Drake promptly slowed the boat and circled.

"Damn!" Mason said.

Watching through the binoculars, Mason could see the boat circling to the rescue, saw the young woman in the water pick up the
end of the rope Drake threw her, then slowly the boat jockeyed
into position and as an arm flashed the signal, Drake once more
gunned the boat and the water skier came erect.

Drake made a series of circles.

Della Street said, "That other boat, the man who was fishing,
seems to be pulling in his anchor and giving up."

"So he does," Mason said. "He's taking a course which will inter-
cept the wake of that boat from the Bancroft house— No, wait a
minute, he's making a wide circle. Here's Drake cutting in front of
him, and the water skier almost flipping water in the fellow's face.
I'll bet he's one angry fisherman."

"Or one exasperated blackmailer," Della Street said.

Drake's boat made another series of circles, then the water skier
gave a signal. Drake slowed the boat. The skier dropped into the
water, then swam gracefully to the boat and another of the young
women came out to put on the water skis.

The second bathing beauty who took up water-skiing was not
as adept as the first, and after about five minutes, she returned to
the boat.

Drake hauled in all of the skiing paraphernalia, made a wide
circle and headed back toward the southern end of the lake and
the public beach.

The man who had been pole fishing in the boat moved slowly
along, then turned and moved back toward a shaded bank, where
he again took up pole fishing. The boat which had put out from
Bancroft's residence returned.

The wind freshened somewhat. There was little traffic on the lake.

Mason searched the waters with his binoculars.

"Can you see any red can?" Della Street asked.

Mason shook his head. "I thought once," he said, "I had a flash of something red, just a brief glimpse of a red dot on the top of a wave. But I can't see a thing now. Drake is returning, so evidently he has completed his mission. Either he's done the job or he hasn't."

"I'll bet he hates to part with those bathing beauties," Della Street said. "This will be right down Drake's alley."

"He'll telephone," Mason said, "and let us know what has happened."

The butler came out with another round of cooling drinks.

The breeze abruptly died away and the surface of the lake became placid. The shore line seemed to drowse in an afternoon stupor.

The Elliott butler, plainly curious but concealing his curiosity as best he could, asked if he could serve them anything else.

"No, thank you," Mason said. "I think we're about finished."

"Yes, sir. Would you care to come inside, sir? It's air-conditioned and quite comfortable."

"No, thanks," Mason said. "We'll wait here."

"But sometimes it's quite warm in the afternoon on the porch, on this side of the lake. There's a more shaded angle around the corner on the other side."

"No, thanks," Mason said. "We're quite comfortable here."

"Yes, sir. Very good, sir."

The butler withdrew.

Some twenty minutes later, the phone rang.

"For you, sir," the butler said to Mason.

Mason took the telephone.

Paul Drake's voice came over the wire. "Perry?"

"Yes."

"Got it."

"Any trouble?"

"No."

"Anyone see you?"

"I don't think so. The young woman who was doing the water-skiing was most adept. She made a flop in the water at just the right time and managed to make the substitution."

"Where in the world was she carrying the can?" Mason asked.

"You'd be surprised."

"No, I'm serious," Mason said. "I'm wondering if she wasn't detected."

"It was in a fake swivel on the ski rope," Drake said. "It was specially fixed up for the purpose."

"And what was in the can?" Mason asked.

"The blackmail note, fifteen hundred dollars in money and ten silver dollars."

"All right," Mason said. "Wait until I get there. Don't do a thing until I arrive."

Mason hung up the telephone and nodded to Della. They thanked the butler, left the Elliott summer mansion, and drove at once to the public launching ramp at the south side of the lake.

Paul Drake met him.

Mason said, "Now, Paul, what *you* have to do is simple."

"Okay," Drake said. "What do we do?"

"You have a starlet there?"

"I'll say we have. Boy, she's a knockout!"

"And she wants publicity?"

"She'd stand on her head and wiggle her feet at the camera for publicity. That's the breath of life to a starlet like this."

"Okay," Mason said. He took a portable typewriter from the back of the automobile and set it up on his lap. "Let's see the can, Paul."

Drake produced the red coffee can with the silver dollars in the bottom and the fifteen hundred dollars in bills and blackmail note on top. Mason took the note, ratcheted it into the typewriter, crossed out the figure, "fifteen hundred" and, over it, wrote "three thousand."

Then the lawyer took fifteen hundred dollars in ten- and twenty-dollar bills from his brief case, added it to the money in the can, replaced the note, and handed the can back to Drake.

"You rented the boat under an assumed name?"

"I did better than that," Drake said. "The boat never came from here at all. I picked it up from a friend and carried it down on a trailer. We simply paid a one-dollar launching fee to use the ramp. I've taken the boat out and we're all ready to go."

"All right," Mason said. "Give this can and the note to the starlet and tell her to contact the lifeguard at the bathing beach and tell him that while she was water-skiing she picked up this coffee can because she thought it was a hazard to navigation. She took off the cover, looked inside and saw it was full of money, then she found this note.

"If the lifeguard doesn't telephone the sheriff's office, be sure that the starlet does . . . What's her name, by the way?"

"Eve Amory."

"You can count on her?"

"Give her publicity and you can count on her until hell freezes over," Drake said. "Publicity is the one thing she wants. She drove down in her own car so she can be independent of us."

"Okay," Mason said, "she's going to get *lots* of publicity."

"Of course," Drake pointed out, "with a setup like this, the newspapers will think it's some kind of a press agent's stunt."

"Have her do *exactly* as I say," Mason said, "and the money will guarantee her good faith."

"What does she do with all this dough?" Drake asked.

"Turns it over to the police," Mason said.

"The whole business?"

"The whole business."

"That's going to hurt," Drake said. "This gal is—"

"That's exactly it," Mason interrupted. "She's hungry. She's operating on a shoestring. The fact that she'll turn three thousand dollars over to the police is indicative of good faith, and the fact that it isn't a publicity stunt. No half-hungry actress would put up three thousand bucks just to get her picture in the paper."

"Okay," Drake said, "you know what you're doing."

"Now, here's her story," Mason said. "She gets dressed, she goes to the lifeguard, she tells him the story. She doesn't know the last names of the people with whom she was boating. She was out with a friend, but he wouldn't want to have his name brought into it. The girls wanted to water-ski. She was teaching them some of the fine points. The girls were actresses or would-be actresses."

"I understand," Drake said. "She'll give the impression that she was out with a potential sugar daddy who was willing to be the angel for a girlie show."

"She's willing to go for that?" Mason asked.

"She'll go for anything, provided she gets her picture in the paper in a bikini bathing suit."

"If I'm any judge of newspapers," Mason said, "the reporters will want her to pose just the way she was when she found the can."

"You think the reporters will go for this?"

"I think so," Mason said. "By the way, Paul, what became of the decoy coffee can that she planted?"

Drake shook his head. "I'll be damned if I know, Perry."

Mason said, "There was a fellow pole fishing in a boat. He started up his boat about the time that boat put out from the Bancroft house."

"I know he did," Drake said, "but I swear he didn't get up to where that can was."

"Well, what happened to the can?"

"It disappeared."

"It did what?"

"It disappeared," Drake said.

"What do you mean, it disappeared?"

"It was floating there for a while and I saw it, both with my naked eye and through the binoculars. Then I pulled in the water-skiing outfit and looked for it again, and the thing was gone."

"What boats had been near there?"

"There wasn't a boat. The thing simply disappeared."

"You mean it sank?" Mason asked.

"It must have."

"But didn't you have the cover put on tight?"

"That's the trouble, Perry. That's where I'm afraid we may have slipped up on the thing. We had to make that substitution awfully fast. This girl was in the water. She took a spill just at the psychological time and in the right place. She grabbed this coffee can and put it in the hollow swivel container I put on the ski rope. Then she put out the substitute coffee can. Now, all I can think of is that the lid of that substitute can must have hit against the water ski when we dumped it and let enough water in so the can sank."

"That," Mason said, "is going to be bad."

"I know," Drake said. "I'm sorry about it, but it's one of those things that you can't help."

"But no other boat tried to cut in, tried to get near that coffee can?"

Drake shook his head. "No other boat. There were some over on the far side of the bank. There were some other water skiers. There was this fellow fishing. No one else was near."

Mason said, "I can't figure it, unless the blackmailers had you spotted as a detective and were afraid to make a try for the coffee can with you hanging around."

"I don't think so," Drake said. "I was wearing those wind goggles and a cap, and I kept pretty well down in the boat."

"Pretty well down and pretty well surrounded with women," Mason said.

"Well," Drake said grinning, "what would *you* have done?"

Mason grinned back at him, said, "Okay, Paul. Get your boat out of there, let the starlet get dressed and go to the lifeguard. . . . Now, you say she has her own transportation?"

"That's right. I had her drive her car down and join us at the landing ramp. There are only twenty-three more payments to make and it's all hers."

"All right," Mason said. "Now, I want the names of everyone who rented boats at the marina this afternoon, and you've had an operative getting the license numbers of every boat that was launched from private automobiles?"

"That's right," Drake said. "I have a man here. He's got the license numbers of the cars and the trailers and the license numbers of the boats."

"All right," Mason said. "Tell him to clear out and go home so the police don't spot him."

"And this whole can of money goes to the police?"

"Every cent of it," Mason said.

"Perhaps someone will give Eve Amory a reward," Drake said. "I'll tell her there's a possibility of that."

"You tell her to keep her bikini bathing suit handy," Mason said. "That's all *she* needs to do."

4

Perry Mason entered his office at nine-thirty.

"Hi, Della," he said. "What's new?"

"You have a very, very irate client in the outer office," she said.

"Harlow Bissinger Bancroft?" Mason asked.

She nodded.

Mason grinned. "Let him come in."

Della Street went to the door and a moment later returned with Bancroft.

"Mason," Bancroft said, "what the devil's this?"

"What?" Mason asked.

Bancroft flung down a morning paper.

Featured on the front page was the photograph of a young woman in a very abbreviated bathing suit and the caption: BATHING BEAUTY FINDS FORTUNE.

"Well, well, well," Mason said.

"What the hell!" Bancroft said. "I trusted you to use discretion. What's the idea of raising the ante from fifteen hundred dollars to three thousand? And this business of a woman almost naked?"

Bancroft whipped over a page and said, "Here you are—a photostatic copy of the blackmail note. My God, that thing was to be handled in the strictest confidence."

"Well, well, well," Mason said, "what do you know."

"What do *I* know!" Bancroft shouted at him. "What do *you* know? You were supposed to handle this thing discreetly."

"Your stepdaughter tossed the can and the blackmail note overboard?" Mason asked.

"I suppose so, I haven't asked her about it. She hasn't seen fit to confide in me, and I certainly haven't asked *her* any questions. But here's the whole blackmail note spread out in the public press and the demand has been raised to three thousand dollars!"

Mason grinned. "Eve Amory certainly got good coverage, didn't she?"

"It depends on what you call coverage," Bancroft snorted. "That bathing suit is just as near to nothing as the law allows. You'd think this was some nudist magazine."

"Oh, she's a long way from being nude," Mason said, reading the account thoughtfully. "What do you know!" he said at length.

"What do *I* know?" Bancroft told him. "I know that I feel I've been let down. I trusted your discretion. I trusted your integrity, and I certainly wanted certain aspects of the matter kept discreetly confidential."

"It's confidential," Mason said.

"Confidential?" Bancroft said, putting the paper on the desk and pounding it with his fist. "God knows how many million readers are going to see this! They tell me it's been picked up by the wire services and will be syndicated in half the newspapers in the country."

"It does make quite a story, doesn't it," Mason said.

"Is that the best you can say?" Bancroft said.

Mason said, "Sit down, Bancroft, and cool off. Now, let me tell you something."

Bancroft slowly sat down, glowering at the lawyer.

"In the first place," Mason said, "publicity is the one thing you wanted to avoid."

"I'm glad you're telling me," Bancroft said sarcastically.

"And, in the second place," Mason said, "publicity is the one thing a blackmailer *has* to avoid. He can only work under cover and surreptitiously.

"Now then, quite obviously the blackmailer's victim didn't go to the police. The victim did exactly as the blackmailer had instructed. The money was placed in the can, the can was tossed overboard, presumably in accordance with instructions that had been given as to time and place. Therefore, the blackmailer can't accuse his victim of bad faith."

"The thing I don't understand," Bancroft said, "is how it happened that ante got doubled. When I saw that note, the demand was for fifteen hundred dollars. Now, you saw that note—in fact, you photographed it. Now, how the devil did the blackmailer increase the demand to three thousand dollars?"

"I did that," Mason said.

"You what?"

"I increased the demand to three thousand," Mason said.

"But my stepdaughter drew fifteen hundred out of the bank and presumably that was all she had to put in the coffee can. Yet, according to police, the sum of three thousand dollars, together with this note and the ten silver dollars was in the can."

Mason grinned slowly at Bancroft.

Bancroft started to say something, then, at the lawyer's grin, his expression suddenly changed.

"Good Lord!" he exclaimed.

"Exactly," Mason said. "This note was written on a Monarch portable typewriter. I secured an old Monarch and crossed out the fifteen-hundred-dollar demand and made it three thousand dollars. Then after we picked up the can, we added fifteen hundred dollars to it, so that it made a total of three thousand."

"*You* put in fifteen hundred dollars?" Bancroft asked.

"Of your money," Mason told him, still grinning. "That's why I told you the expenses would be high."

"But what— You mean . . . ?"

Mason said, "I am assuming that this was at least a two-man job. You'll notice the note says, 'we.' Of course, that may have been simply a blind, but somehow I don't think it was.

"Now, suppose you were part of a criminal conspiracy and you had a partner. You sent him out to collect fifteen hundred dollars blackmail money. The collection was bungled and the police got hold of the money. But by the time the police received the money, it turned out the ante had been boosted to three thousand dollars. Wouldn't you naturally assume that your partner had double-crossed you and tried to raise an extra fifteen hundred that he was going to hold out on you? And if you reached such an assumption, would the denial of your partner do any good?

"I think we may safely assume that with the publication of this note, we have put the blackmailers on the defensive, and with the fact that the amount in the can actually was three thousand dollars instead of fifteen hundred, we have sowed the seeds of potential discord."

"Well, I'll be damned," Bancroft said.

"Furthermore," Mason told him, "I think we're going to get a line on the blackmailers. And once we do that, I'm going to try to keep them occupied with something to think about."

"Such as what?" Bancroft asked.

"Oh," Mason said, "we'll think up things to keep them busy. The trouble with blackmailers is that, while they make their living out of skeletons which are in other people's closets, they necessarily have to have a whole closetful of their own skeletons. Unless they are rank amateurs, they must necessarily have been making their living out of crime and out of blackmail. That leaves a back trail that bothers them, in case the police should pick it up."

Bancroft slowly got to his feet. "Mason," he said, "I owe you an apology. The more I think of it, that's the cleverest damned move, the most daring move, and the most skillful move anybody could possibly dream up. You've put the shoe on the other foot and— damn it, it's well worth the three thousand dollars."

"Hold everything," Mason said. "You haven't lost a penny of the three thousand dollars yet. It isn't in the custody of the blackmailers, it's in the custody of the police.

"Now then, what would *you* do if you were a blackmailer? Would you go to the police and say, 'I'm sorry, sir, but that money was intended for me'?"

"No, of course not," Bancroft said. "But they will, of course, make other demands."

"Sure, they'll make other demands," Mason said, "but they'd have made other demands anyway. And when they make other demands, we'll find some way of dealing with those demands."

Bancroft reached out and gripped the lawyer's hand. "Mason," he said, "you go ahead, you play this your own way. You call on me for anything you want."

"I warned you," Mason said, "that I wouldn't play this in a conventional manner."

"You warned me," Bancroft said, "and you sure as hell meant what you said. . . . Do you want some more money?"

"Not yet," Mason told him. "At the proper time, I'll get that money back from the police."

"How?"

"When I sent my secretary down to the bank to get some money in ten- and twenty-dollar bills," Mason said, "I gave her a check for three thousand dollars, which she cashed in tens and twenties. I put fifteen hundred dollars in the safe and took fifteen hundred dollars to plant in that coffee can. At the proper time, I'll tell the police that the money that was put in the can was bait for a blackmailer and show them my canceled check for three thousand dollars to prove it, with a statement from the banker that the money was paid to my secretary in tens and twenties."

Bancroft paused for a moment, thinking that over, then suddenly threw back his head and laughed.

He started for the exit door, turned and said, "Mason, when I came into this office I was breathing fire. I'm going out walking on air."

"Don't be too sure of yourself yet," Mason said. "You aren't out of the woods, but we're starting a backfire and the blackmailers are going to have to watch out they don't get burned."

"I'll say they're going to have to watch out," Bancroft said.

When the door had closed behind him, Mason pulled the paper over and grinned at the photograph of Eve Amory.

"There are more photographs on the back page," Della Street said, "photographs showing her on the water skis, showing what happened when she fell in the water and saw the red coffee can floating nearby. Chief, what's going to happen to her?"

"She'll probably get a pretty darned good contract," Mason said.

"But she's going to be in danger."

"Sure, she's going to be in danger," Mason said. "And, as her attorney, I'm going to see she gets protection. Unless I'm greatly mistaken, somebody is going to telephone her, making an anonymous threat."

5

At ten-thirty, Paul Drake's code knock sounded on the door of Mason's office.

Della Street let him in.

"Well," the detective said, perching himself on a corner of Mason's desk, "you certainly got publicity."

"Eve Amory got publicity," Mason said.

"And that isn't all," Drake said. "The newspapers went for this lock, stock and barrel, just as you said. At first, they thought it was some kind of publicity stunt, but the three thousand bucks in tens and twenties was a stage prop that no press agent could afford. So they figured it was genuine."

Mason nodded. "How does Eve feel?"

Drake grinned and said, "Eve feels on the top of cloud nine. She's being asked to make a television appearance tonight on one of the newscaster's shows."

"What are the police doing?"

"The police have consulted the examiner of questioned documents. He has come up with the information that the typewriter on which the demand was written was a Monarch Ten portable."

Mason grinned.

"And," Drake went on, "the news being quiet at the moment, the newspapers have assigned some of their ace reporters to find out who is being blackmailed. They are acting on the assumption that the victim was someone living along the shores of Lake Merticito and was some wealthy individual. They assume that the coffee can with the money in it was, of course, prepared in accordance with the written instructions and tossed out in the water, pursuant to telephoned instructions, where it was inadvertently picked up by Eve Amory."

"Better and better," Mason said.

31

"Don't be too sure," Drake said. "Those reporters are pretty damned competent individuals. They may start getting pretty close to the truth."

"Whatever the truth is," Mason said.

"Of course," Drake told him, "you haven't confided all the details to me, and I'm not asking you to, but I'm just warning you."

"Thanks," Mason told him. "I will heed it."

Drake said, "Newspaper reporters are combing the public launching ramp, trying to find out who rented boats yesterday and what boats were put in the water. Fortunately, the caretaker there keeps a list of the collections he makes, but he doesn't keep the license numbers of the boats, and so far, I guess we're the only one that has a complete list."

"You have it?" Mason asked.

"My operative checked every boat that went out."

"Who was the man who was doing the pole fishing?"

"Now, that's a peculiar thing," Drake said. "That boat was rented for half a day for fishing to two men."

"Two men?" Mason asked.

"That's right."

"But there was only one man in the boat."

Drake said, "Later on, when the boat was returned, there were two men in it."

"Any names?" Mason asked.

"The man who runs the place doesn't have any names. It was simply a cash rental of a boat with an outboard motor, as far as he was concerned. It was one of those low-powered motors that they use for trolling and fishing, and the boat was a battered-up old hulk that wouldn't make any speed, even with a decent motor on it."

"And what about your man?" Mason asked.

"My man," Drake said, "has a fair description of the two men, but that's all. One of them was in his twenties; the other was around forty-five."

Mason frowned thoughtfully.

Suddenly the lawyer said, "That red coffee can just seemed to disappear while you were looking at it?"

"That's right," Drake said. "I took my eyes off of it for a moment, and when I looked again, it was gone. I suppose the only explanation is that something knocked the lid loose and it filled with water and sank."

Mason shook his head. "We're dealing with people who are cleverer than the average, Paul."

"What do you mean?"

Mason said, "Two men rented that fishing boat. One of them must have had a skin-diving outfit. I'll bet they loaded a great big hamper in the boat and perhaps some other baggage, as well. Then they went out to a certain spot on the lake, the skin diver put on his tanks and slipped overboard.

"The victim had been told to toss the coffee can overboard at a certain time in a certain place."

Drake said, "The boat which put out from the Bancroft residence was operated by one person, a young woman. She tossed the coffee can over and then made a couple of circles with the boat, circling around the coffee can."

"And, at that moment," Mason said, "the skin diver was coming up to pull the coffee can under. In that way, anyone who had been watching wouldn't have seen any other boat near the place. What's more, if police *had* been tipped off, there wouldn't have been the faintest possible clue. At one minute the coffee can would have been floating, and then the next minute it wouldn't have been floating."

"Well, I'll be damned," Drake said, as the full force of the idea struck him."

"But," Mason said, "you suddenly speeded up and came swirling around, cutting didos in the water, and the skin diver was afraid to come up until you got out of there. Then your water skier tipped into the water, juggled the coffee cans— Tell me, Paul, was that Eve Amory who did that?"

"No," Drake said, "that was one of my operatives, one who is an expert water skier. Of course, Eve claims that *she* was the one who made the find. That's the way you instructed me to have it done."

Mason's eyes narrowed. "That boat with the pole fisherman is the solution, Paul. The skin diver waited until you had got out of the vicinity, then he came up and grabbed the red coffee can that you had substituted, went back under water, swam under water to the bank. The pole fisherman put into the bank the skin diver climbed into the boat, changed his clothes and they came back as two innocent fishermen carrying a big hamper."

"And by that time they knew they'd been gypped," Drake said.

"That's right. They were furious, thinking someone had double-crossed them. Then, by this morning, they'll have read the paper and think that it just happened there were two coffee cans floating around and they grabbed the wrong coffee can, and Eve Amory happened to stumble onto the right one."

"And by that time?" Drake asked.

"By that time, one of them will have accused the other one of double-crossing, and there'll be some bad blood."

"And then?" Drake asked.

"From that point on," Mason said, "we'll play it by ear. The main thing is to get them on the defensive and keep them on the defensive."

"And what about the victim in this thing, the one they were putting the bite on?" Drake said. "You can imagine how *she* feels, reading about this in the paper."

"Particularly," Mason said, "when she reads about the fact that there was three thousand dollars in the coffee can."

"The blackmailers will contact her by telephone and she'll say she only put fifteen hundred in," Drake said.

"And that will confirm the blackmailer's idea that someone in the crowd is executing a double-cross, and this girl had been warned to say nothing about it."

"You're putting her in quite a spot," Drake said.

Mason nodded. "So we're going to give her an armed escort at all times, Paul. Only she won't know a thing about it. Put an electric bug on her car. Have at least two and possibly three shadows on her at all times. Put out all the men you need to."

"I don't suppose I need to warn you," Drake said, "that you're playing one hell of a dangerous game. These fellows may mean business."

Mason's face was grim. "I mean business myself, Paul."

6

Shortly before noon, Della Street entered Mason's private office and said, "You are confronted with a problem."

"What?" he asked.

"A very irate Rosena Andrews is in the outer office, with fire in her eye."

"Any idea how she got a lead to me?" Mason asked.

"She isn't talking," Della Street said. "She says she has to see you immediately upon a strictly personal matter of the greatest importance."

Mason grinned and said, "Well, we may as well face it, Della. Let her come in. . . . Is she the type who would pull a gun out of her purse and start shooting, or would she climb across the desk and start clawing?"

"She's the type that might do both," Della Street said. "She's very much a law unto herself, if I'm any judge of character."

"Well, you certainly should be," Mason said, "after having been on the firing line in a law office. Bring her in."

A few moments later, Della Street held the door open and an irate, twenty-three-old woman came marching into the office, her blue eyes snapping with anger.

"You're Perry Mason," she said.

"That's right," Mason told her.

"Well, I'll thank you to keep your hands out of my business! I don't know just what recourse I have, but I certainly intend to take it up with the Bar Association, or anyone else in authority."

Mason raised inquiring eyebrows. "I've been interfering with your business?"

"You know you have."

"Perhaps," Mason said, "you might care to sit down and give me the details."

35

"I don't have to sit down," she said. "That blasted publicity in the paper this morning is enough. I know my stepfather called you yesterday upon an emergency matter and I'm giving you credit for having engineered the whole scheme."

"The *whole* scheme?" Mason asked.

"You know what I mean. The grabbing of the coffee can and changing the note and putting in fifteen hundred dollars more, and— Will you kindly tell me *what* you're trying to do, Mr. Mason?"

Mason smiled tolerantly and said, "Not while you're in this mood, Miss Andrews. If I'm going to talk to you at all, I should like to do so when we could look at the matter with calm appraisal."

"I'm willing to listen," she said.

"With one ear," Mason told her. "You're too indignant to give undivided attention at the present time."

"Well, I have a right to be indignant."

"You still haven't told me why."

"You know perfectly well why. That blackmail note was sent to *me. I* was the one who was instructed to get the fifteen hundred dollars in ten- and twenty-dollar bills, put them in a coffee can with ten silver dollars to balance the coffee can just enough so it would keep floating right side up, put the lid on tight and toss it overboard from my boat at a time when there were no boats in the vicinity.

"No sooner had I done it than this boat with a lot of scantily clad bathing beauties came swooping up out of nowhere—I thought at first they were the people who were going to collect the money, but then I decided they wouldn't be quite that brazen about it. However, there seemed to be no one else in the vicinity, so I let it go."

"Now, let's get this straight," Mason said. "You say the blackmail note was addressed to you?"

"You know it was."

"How would I know?"

"Probably through my stepfather, who has been snooping around and who took that note from my desk and then replaced it under the blotter."

"How do you know that?"

"I took the precaution of marking the exact place I had put the note under the blotter. I just wanted to know if someone might be snooping around."

"Do I gather there is no great amount of affection lost between you and your stepfather?" Mason asked.

"You don't gather anything of the sort. I love him. He's wonderful, considerate, overly protective, overly solicitous, a worrywart, and he's always worrying about me."

"So what do we do now?" Mason asked.

"Now," she said, "I don't know. You've put me on a spot. I had fifteen hundred dollars to turn over to some people who were going to suppress certain information. Somebody has changed the note to three thousand dollars, somebody has put in another fifteen hundred dollars in addition to mine, and now we've got a startlet in a bikini bathing suit having her photograph all over the front pages of the papers, the police have got hold of the money, and— Well, frankly, there's hell to pay."

"Has anybody asked you to pay hell yet?" Mason asked.

"Not yet," she said, "but I dread what's going to happen."

"Perhaps," Mason said, "you'd care to tell me how it happens you're so vulnerable."

"What do you mean, vulnerable?"

"So that a blackmailer could put a bite on you."

"I think we're all vulnerable," she said. "Virtually everybody has some skeleton in his closet."

"What's *your* skeleton?"

"That's none of your business. I realize you're trying to protect me in some way, but I'm here to advise you, Mr. Perry Mason, that I don't want protection. I want to deal with this thing in my own way."

Mason said, "I hope you realize that once you start playing ball with a blackmailer, you're licked. You pay once and then you pay again and then you pay again and again and again, and then you keep on paying until you're bled white."

"No one is going to bleed *me* white," she said. "I'm gaining time, that's all."

"Time for what?"

"Time to play things my own way. I'll take care of my own business in my own way, and I don't need your help."

"Were you," Mason asked, solicitously, "trying to protect some-one else in this thing?"

"That," she said, "is none of your business. All I want to tell you, face to face, is that I want you to keep out of this and let me handle it my own way."

"But don't you understand, you're walking into quicksand," Mason said. "You keep getting deeper and deeper and—"

"I know what I'm doing, Mr. Mason. I'm gaining time. I was willing to pay fifteen hundred dollars to gain time."

"And then they'll put another bite on you."

"By that time," she said viciously, "they'll break their teeth."

"You seem to be a very determined young woman."

"And resourceful," she added. "Don't forget that."

Mason sized her up thoughtfully. "Perhaps if you'd tell me just what you have in mind, Miss Andrews, I might be able to give you some advice that would help and we could, so to speak, pool our resources."

She doggedly shook her head.

"This information that is hinted at in the blackmail letter. You have an idea what that is all about?"

"I *know* what it is all about," she snapped.

"Would you care to discuss it?"

"Certainly not. It's my business and my business alone."

"Perhaps," Mason said, "for romantic reasons, or perhaps because of social prestige, you feel that if you could gain a few days or a few weeks or so, you could handle the situation to better advantage."

"Perhaps," she said.

"Do you think it would make any real difference?" Mason asked.

"What would?"

"The passage of time."

"Yes."

Mason said, "The persons who sent that note have been com-municating with you by telephone?"

"That would seem to be a natural inference."

"Is there any way by which they identify themselves?"

"That," she said, "is something else that I don't care to dis-cuss. . . . The purpose of this visit, Mr. Mason, is to tell you that I don't want your services. I have no need for the services of a lawyer. I am doing this on my own, I have my own plans, I am handling things my own way, and I don't want any interference. I'll thank you, therefore, to keep out of my affairs entirely and completely. And this is formal notice."

With that, she turned and marched abruptly out of the office.

Mason nodded to Della Street. "See if you can get Bancroft on the phone for me."

A few moments later, Della Street nodded to Perry Mason and said, "He's on the line."

"Hello, Bancroft," Mason said. "I've just received a visit from your stepdaughter. She's breathing smoke and fire."

"How in the world did she find out about you?"

"Apparently she knew you called me yesterday morning and came dashing in for an emergency appointment. She also felt certain that you had read the blackmail note while she was out of her room. You changed the position of the note somewhat."

"Just what did Rosena want?" Bancroft asked.

"She wanted to serve notice on me personally and professionally that she didn't need any attorney, that she was fully capable of taking care of herself, that she had her own plans and that she didn't want any interference from me."

"I don't care *what* she said," Bancroft said, "you stay on the job! She's young and impulsive and self-reliant—too self-reliant. She thinks she can cope with professional blackmailers and she can't do it."

Mason said, "It might be a good plan if you went to her and had a frank talk, inasmuch as she knows you saw the letter, and inasmuch as she's trying to protect you as well as herself. You might do well to sit down and discuss it with her."

"No," Bancroft said, "she has to come to me. She's got to break the ice. So far, she hasn't seen fit to confide in me, but this blackmail letter was intended for her and she's playing her cards close to her chest. I'm not going to interfere."

"In view of the fact that she has told me to keep the hell out of her affairs," Mason said, "my hands are somewhat tied."

"What do you mean, somewhat?"

"Well, I can't represent *her* in any way."

"You don't have to," Bancroft said. "You're representing me. I'm trying to keep this matter from becoming public. I *have* to keep it from becoming public. I have every right on earth to retain you as my attorney. You're doing fine so far. You've got the other people on the defensive. Stay with it. . . . Do you want any more money?"

"Not yet."

"Any time you need any more, just call on me," Bancroft said. "Frankly, Mason, the more I think of it, I'm tickled to death with developments. I can see the thing from the viewpoint of the enemy camp—but I don't want Rosena put in any position that will endanger her."

"Okay," Mason said, "we'll carry on the best we can."

"Suppose the blackmailers think she double-crossed them?"

"They won't. They'll feel one of the gang tried to cut himself in for an extra fifteen-hundred-buck slice of cake. That will be their first reaction. Your stepdaughter did everything the note told her to do. They'll feel they just happened to grab an empty can instead of the right one, and, in the face of all this publicity, they'll be jittery."

"Just the same, I'm worrying about Rosena's safety."

"Don't," Mason said. "She has an armed bodyguard at all times."

"Does she know it?"

"Not yet."

"Will she find it out?"

"She may."

"When she does there'll be trouble."

"We'll face that when we come to it," Mason told him. "By that time it's almost certain that there will be other developments that will take precedence."

"Okay," Bancroft said. "You're the doctor. However, there's one thing you should know. Rosena is a very determined young woman, and she has armed herself."

"She's *what?*" Mason demanded.

"She has armed herself. At least I think she has. Either Rosena or Phyllis, my wife, has taken the .38-caliber revolver I keep in the dresser drawer by the side of my bed."

"How do you know?"

"Because I went to the dresser a few minutes ago to get the gun. I made up my mind I might as well have it handy—and it was gone. It has to be either Rosena or Phyllis who has it."

"How long since you've seen it?" Mason asked.

"Why, I keep it there all the time."

"How long since you've actually *seen* it?"

"Well . . . now, I don't know, perhaps a week or so."

"Where's your wife now?"

"Back in town—at our apartment there. She's still working on that charity shindig."

"Perhaps you'd better get in here yourself," Mason said. "A little family conference might not be amiss at this time."

"I want them to come to me," Bancroft said. "It's a matter where they have to take the initiative."

"You'd better come in," Mason told him, "before Rosena takes the initiative with *your* gun."

"Heavens, I hadn't thought of that," Bancroft said.

"Think of it now, then," Mason told him, and hung up.

7

At three o'clock in the afternoon Della said, "This seems to be your day for troubled women."

"Who is it now?" Mason asked.

"The starlet, Eve Amory, and she's certainly upset. I wouldn't be too surprised if she hadn't been doing a little crying."

"The devil!" Mason said. "Let's see her."

"You have an appointment in a few minutes and—"

"The appointment can wait," Mason said. "This girl may be in serious trouble. Incidentally, find out from Paul if he has a shadow on her and if he hasn't, be sure that someone tails her when she leaves the office—a good, husky, two-fisted individual who can keep an eye on her and act as bodyguard. And tell me a little more about Eve before you bring her in, Della."

"She's very, very beautiful," Della Street said. "She'd make anyone stop and do a double-take."

"What else?" Mason asked.

"Well," Della Street said critically, "I don't want to be catty, but after the double-take you feel that you've seen it all, that you've looked at the entire inventory."

"What do you mean?"

"She doesn't have the individuality, the spontaneity. She does everything in too rehearsed a manner. She smiles and holds the smile just a second too long, as though she had been practicing it in front of a mirror. When she stands, when she walks, when she moves, you get that feeling of synthetic charm. You don't feel that you're getting through to the girl herself."

"Well, I'll take a look and check your observations," Mason said.

"You'll take a look and fall overboard," Della said. "It'll be a while before you are able to make a calm appraisal. She's *very* beautiful."

"Bring her in," Mason said. "Let's see what's on her mind. And be

sure to call Paul Drake and tell him that I want her shadowed, not
so much to see where she goes, but for her own protection. I want
somebody keeping an eye on her who can get tough if he has to.
Now go bring her in, Della, and let me be properly dazzled."

Della Street left the office to return in a few moments with Eve
Amory.

"Well," Mason said, smiling, "I've seen your picture in the papers."

She smiled, and held the smile for a full second too long. Then
she gave Mason her hand and said, "That's what I wanted to see
you about."

"Why me?" Mason asked.

"The man with whom I was working," she said, "was Paul Drake.
He's a private detective. I learned that he handles your business
and I know that he reported to you after we had picked up the can
with the money in it."

"How do you know that?" Mason asked curiously.

"I'm not blind, and after all, Mr. Mason, you are not entirely un-
known. Your picture has been in the papers . . ." She smiled and
added, "Even more than mine."

"Go on," Mason said.

She said, "I have been contacted by a very suave, ruthless individual who has put me in very much of a spot."

"What kind of a spot?" Mason asked.

"This individual," she said, "knows something about me."

"You have a past?" Mason asked.

She met his eyes and said, "Every aspiring Hollywood actress who
is beautiful enough to want a future could very well have a past.
And a present."

"And what about this individual?" Mason asked.

"He was a man about fifty—perhaps forty-five to fifty-two. He
has penetrating gray eyes, and he has a single-track mind."

"What do you mean by that?" Mason asked. "You mean that he
wants to—"

"No, no," she interrupted hastily, "I mean just the opposite, Mr.
Mason. He is not influenced in the least by feminine wiles, charm,
tears, smiles or nylon."

"Go on," Mason said. "What does he want?"

"Money."

"How much money?"

"The three thousand dollars I found."

"You turned the three thousand dollars over to the police," Mason said. "Doesn't this man read the papers?"

"This man reads the papers," she said. "This man does more than that. He gets around."

"And what did he want?" Mason asked.

"He wants the three thousand."

"How does he expect to get it?"

"The only way he could get it. I am to make a statement to the police that this whole thing was a setup for publicity, that a friend staked me to the three thousand dollars and the blackmail note and the idea was that I would go water-skiing in a very scanty bathing suit and claim that I'd found the money and the note in a coffee can and the inference would be that one of the wealthy families living along the shores of the lake was being blackmailed and the newspapers would give me a lot of personal publicity.

"He said I was to break down and confess to the police that that's all it was, a campaign for personal publicity, a press-agent stunt that the newspapers fell for. Then he said in the course of time the police would have to give me back the three thousand dollars and I could turn it over to him."

"Or else?" Mason asked.

"Oh, of course," she said, "there was an 'or else.' And it's something that bothers me very much because it would look rather bad in print."

Mason studied her thoughtfully. "You feel that your career requires you have nothing in your past?" he asked.

She said, "I don't care a fig for myself, but this involves someone else. A man who is the father of two children."

"Did this man who called on you give you his name?"

She shook her head. "He said that I could refer to him as 'Mr. X.'"

"And how were you to get in touch with him?"

"I wasn't. He was going to get in touch with me."

Mason said, "This evidently bothers you."

"It bothers me a lot."

Mason said, "If you should come out now and make a statement of that sort and claim that this was all a publicity gag, and that the newspapers had fallen for it, you'd incur the undying enmity of a lot of reporters."

"I know it."

"It would quite probably kill any career you might have in store for you."

"You don't need to spell these things out for me, Mr. Mason."

"Yet you still feel that you might be forced to make such a statement?"

"I can't help thinking of the man and the children."

"The man, I take it, is rather powerful in certain circles?"

"Very."

"What does he have to say about it?"

"I haven't told him."

"Why not?"

"It would throw him into a tailspin—and of course I don't know how much Mr. X knows and how much of what he claimed he knew was based on bluff. I've been seen with this man in public a couple of times and— Well, it could be all a legitimate business relationship or it could be something else."

Mason thought for a moment, then said, "When is this man going to get in touch with you again?"

"Sometime this evening."

Mason said, "All right, tell him that he has a nice scheme but it won't do a damned bit of good, that an attorney is willing to swear that it was a genuine deal involving blackmail."

She thought that over for a moment. "Could I tell him the name of the attorney?"

"You're damned right you can tell him the name of the attorney," Mason said. "Tell him it's Perry Mason and tell him to come and see me."

She was silent for several seconds, thinking the thing over. Then she abruptly gave Perry Mason her hand.

"That," she said, "ought to do it."

Mason said, "I don't like blackmailers. They're human vultures who prey on other people's weaknesses and their desire to avoid publicity. You tell your Mr. X if he wants to discuss it further to come and see me personally."

"No," she said thoughtfully, "I think the minute I mention your name and tell him that you are willing to swear the money in the coffee can was really blackmail money he'll start running for cover."

Mason said, "I just want you to know that we appreciate your co-operation in this."

She smiled and again her smile was held just a fraction of a second too long.

"It has turned out to be a very good thing for me, Mr. Mason, and I thank you. Do I go out the same way I came in or . . . ?"

"No, out this door," Mason said.

When she had left the office Mason nodded to Della Street who promptly got Paul Drake on the line.

"You've got someone tagging Eve Amory?" Mason asked.

"That's right. I've had somebody on her for half an hour. He tailed her up to the building here. I thought she was coming to see me. Instead of that she detoured in to see you folks."

"She was approached by a rather suave individual somewhere in his fifties," Mason said.

"That was before my man got on the job," Drake said. "We don't have anything like that in the report."

"Keep an eye out for him," Mason said, "and if you can find him, tail him. I think he's going to come back sometime later on in the afternoon or in the early part of the evening."

"Who is he?" Drake asked.

"He gives the name of Mr. X," Mason said, "and unless I'm greatly mistaken, he's the blackmailer. He's around forty-five to fifty-two with penetrating gray eyes and—"

"That'll be the man who was doing pole fishing in the boat," Drake said. "We've got a pretty good description of him."

"Okay," Mason said. "Now we're getting in touch with the blackmailers and once we find out who they are we'll take the initiative and give them something to think of.

"Stay on the job, Paul."

8

Shortly after four o'clock Della picked up the phone in response to a ring from the receptionist and listened with growing consternation depicted on her face.

"What is it?" Mason asked, as Della cupped her hand over the mouthpiece and turned to face him.

"Now," she said, "we've come full circle. Mrs. Harlow Bancroft is in the office and insists that she has to see you at once upon a matter of the greatest importance."

"Have her wait just a minute," Mason said, "and rush through a call to Harlow Bancroft. Try him at the lake house. If he isn't there, try his office."

Della said into the telephone, "She'll have to wait for just a few minutes, Gertie. It won't be long. Explain that to her, please, and then give me an outside line."

Della waited until she was connected with an outside line, then dialed the number of Harlow Bancroft's lake house. After a moment she said, "may I speak with Mr. Bancroft, please? Tell him it is quite important. This is Mr. Mason's secretary. . . . Oh, I see. Do you know where I can reach him? Thank you, I'll try the office. I have the number. Thank you."

She hung up, said to Mason, "He's not there. The person who answered thinks he may be at the office."

"Try that number," Mason said.

Again Della dialed and again repeated the message that Mr. Mason's office was calling Mr. Bancroft on a matter of the greatest importance.

Again, after a pause, she said, "Thank you. Do you know where we can reach him? . . . Thank you."

Della hung up and said, "The lake house thinks he's at the office, the office thinks we might get him at his lake house."

Mason sighed. "All right," he said. "Tell Mrs. Bancroft to come in. I'm going to have to play it by ear."

"What are you going to tell her?"

"Nothing," Mason said. "I can't tell her that her husband has consulted me because he hasn't given me permission to tell her, and at the same time, I'm not going to lie about it."

Della nodded, went to the outer office and returned with Mrs. Harlow Bancroft.

There was an air of regal poise about Mrs. Bancroft. She was obviously somewhat younger than her husband and the type who looked younger than her age; a woman who took care of her figure and made it a point of pride to watch the details of her personal appearance.

"Good afternoon, Mr. Mason," she said. "I've heard a lot about you. I've seen your picture many times and I'm glad to have this opportunity to meet you face to face. You are, I believe, acting as attorney for my husband?"

Mason raised his eyebrows. "You got that information from your husband?" he asked.

"No."

"May I ask where you did get it?"

"From my daughter."

"I have had a visit from your daughter," Mason said. "She had assumed certain things to be true and had acted upon that assumption."

"Very well, Mr. Mason, I won't ask you to commit yourself. We will take it on that basis. I am going to assume certain things to be true, and act upon that assumption.

"I want to state that neither my daughter nor my husband knows that I am here."

Mason said, "Obviously if I were acting as attorney for your husband I could hardly keep such a visit confidential, and if I am not acting as your husband's attorney I would definitely not want you to commit yourself by—"

"Oh, stop it," she interrupted. "I appreciate your position. I'm trying to respect it. Now, if I may, I'll sit down and tell you a few things in the utmost confidence."

"You are not asking me to act as *your* attorney?" Mason asked.

"No, I simply want you to know certain things."

"Very well. I'm a good listener."

"And your secretary?"

"Is a very good listener and a very poor talker," Mason said.

"All right, I'm going to begin at the beginning. My daughter, Rosena, is engaged to Jetson Blair. The Blair family, as you know, is very prominent socially—you might say 'blue-blooded aristocrats.' Commercially they've failed to distinguish themselves but they maintain a high social status.

"My husband has proven to be a very good businessman."

"And a good provider?" Mason asked.

"A *very* good provider."

"Go on," Mason said.

She said, "Jetson Blair is twenty-four. He had a brother two years younger, Carleton Rasmus Blair, who was a little wild. In fact, he got into all sorts of trouble and much of it was hushed up. He joined the army, went into aviation and took off on an observation trip from which the plane failed to return.

"He was first reported as missing. It was more than a year before the plane was finally found. It had crashed on a mountainside. Apparently there had been no survivors but they were not able to account for all of the personnel. Some of them had evidently been killed by the crash; some of them had apparently been badly injured. Exposure to weather and the depredations of wild animals had made definite identification virtually impossible.

"Carleton, who had been listed as missing, was subsequently listed as having been killed."

Mason merely nodded.

"A couple of years ago," she went on, "a man by the name of Irwin Victor Fordyce was convicted of a crime and sent to San Quentin. He was released a few weeks ago. More recently there was a holdup of a service station and, following a usual pattern of procedure, the police gave the victims of the holdup an opportunity to look through what are known in the vernacular as mug shots—the pictures of criminals who have recently been released from custody and the pictures of persons whose modus operandi is such that there would be a definite possibility of involvement.

"One of the victims made a tentative identification of Irwin Fordyce as one of the holdup men."

Mason's face showed his keen interest.

"Go on," he said.

At this point Mrs. Bancroft weighed her words carefully. "I have been told," she said, "that because Carleton Blair was officially declared dead, his fingerprints were placed in a closed file. I have also been told that Carleton was not killed, but managed to reach a trapper's cabin where he found some provisions, nursed himself back to health, and then being fed up with army life and realizing that he had made something of a failure in life, decided to let Carleton R. Blair vanish forever. He chose the alias of Irwin Victor Fordyce and eventually made his way back to civilization, where he got in trouble and was sentenced to San Quentin.

"Obviously, Mr. Mason, the fact that one of the socially prominent Blairs had served a term in prison and was even now being sought by the police in connection with a service-station holdup would be rather a poor background for a wedding."

"Your daughter told you this?" Mason asked.

"My daughter did not. The information was given to me by a blackmailer."

"What did this blackmailer want?" Mason asked.

"What would you presume he wanted? Money, of course."

Mason's eyes narrowed. He started to say something, then checked himself.

After a few moments of silence Mrs. Bancroft went on, "Naturally, this was at a very crucial period in my daughter's life."

"In other words, you paid?" Mason asked.

"I paid."

"How much?"

"A thousand dollars."

Mason's fingertips drummed on the edge of the desk.

"It wasn't until I read the papers that I realized that a separate and presumably a simultaneous demand had also been made on my daughter—and I wouldn't be too surprised if a demand hadn't been made upon my husband."

"And how about the Blairs?"

"If any demand has been made upon them, nothing has been said about it. The Blairs are not poor people by any means, but on the other hand they are not affluent."

"They would certainly be able to pay a relatively small amount of blackmail at a time like this," Mason said.

"I would assume so."

"Can you," Mason asked, "give me a description of the black-mailer? Was he a man with penetrating gray eyes, perhaps fifty years old and—"

She shook her head. "No, he was a young man. Not over twenty-five or twenty-six. A rather good-looking chap with a crew haircut, dark eyes, broad shoulders, but somewhat coarse features."

"And you paid him a thousand dollars?"

"Yes."

"How?"

"In a package of tens and twenties."

"He assured you there would be no further blackmail?"

"He assured me that I had purchased his silence."

"He must have shown you some proof," Mason said, "something that—"

"Oh, certainly. He had the police photographs of Irwin Fordyce, his fingerprints and measurements. He had photographs of Carleton Blair taken before he joined the army, and I must admit there was a remarkable resemblance. In addition to which he had a set of fingerprints which he claimed were the fingerprints of Carleton R. Blair taken when he joined the army."

"Did you report any of this to your daughter?"

"Certainly not. This is a period of happiness for my daughter. I don't want it spoiled."

"Did you say anything to your husband?"

"Certainly not."

"Why not?"

"He has enough problems of his own."

Mason said, "Didn't it occur to you that the blackmailers would call on your daughter and probably call on your husband?"

"No."

"Why," Mason asked, "do you come to me now?"

"Because," she said, "you've entered the picture and have stirred everything up."

"In what way?"

"You know what you've done. Now then, Mr. Mason, these black-mailers are trying to get in touch with my daughter so that they can make additional demands upon her."

"You say they are trying to get in touch with her?"

"I'll put it this way," she said. "They have contacted her on the telephone."

"How do you know?"

"Because I listened in on a telephone extension."

"And what was the conversation?"

"The man said that she had betrayed them, and my daughter either thought the man who was telephoning was a newspaper reporter or was smart enough to pretend that she did.

"My daughter said that she certainly had no comment to make to the press and that she assumed that the man at the other end of the line was a newspaper reporter who was making it his business to call up every person residing along the lake and run a good bluff, hoping that someone would make some statement which would give the newspapers a clue as to the blackmail victim.

"She said that she thoroughly resented such tactics, that whoever the person was who was being blackmailed it was his or her own business and she thought that the press had sunk to a new low when it tried to ferret out the private affairs of reputable citizens and blazon them all over the front pages of the newspapers; that that was journalism at its lowest and that she just wanted this reporter at the other end of the line to know what she felt about it."

"And then?" Mason asked.

"Then she slammed the phone down."

Mason said, "That would be quite a gambit. It would put a blackmailer on the defensive. How did you know that your daughter was being blackmailed? Did she confide in you?"

"She did not, but I knew she had made a short spin in our speedboat. I also learned that she had asked for a red coffee can. Then when I read the newspaper account featuring the money and the blackmail note I realized, of course, what had happened."

"But you said nothing to her?"

"No."

"And she has said nothing to you about this?"

"No."

"But you did listen in on the telephone conversation?" Mason said.

"I thought that the blackmailers might try to get in touch with her and I wanted to see what was happening."

"Specifically why do you come to me?"

"Because I think my daughter may be in danger; because I feel that my husband has undoubtedly consulted you, and because you are playing with dynamite and I want you to know all of the hidden potentials."

"And you have had a direct contact with one of the blackmailers."

"I have had a direct contact with a young man who specifically wanted blackmail in order to keep from broadcasting the information that he had."

"How was he going to broadcast it?"

"He said one of the scandal magazines would be only too glad to pay him a thousand dollars for the story. That was why he fixed the price at a thousand dollars. He said that he needed the money, that he didn't want to stoop to making money in that way, but he needed it; that he would much rather receive the same amount for suppressing the information. He sounded very convincing."

"Do you intend to tell your husband about this?" Mason asked.

"No."

"Do I have your permission to tell him about it?"

"No. I am simply giving you information which I feel you should have."

"Has it occurred to you that you may be in some danger yourself?"

"Danger," she said, "from blackmailers? Pooh! They are cowards, Mr. Mason. This man extorted a thousand dollars from me, I assume that he had a confederate who extorted three thousand dollars from my daughter. I think the matter would have stopped there if it hadn't been for all this spectacular publicity and the fact that the three thousand dollars the blackmailers had counted on getting from my daughter wound up in the hands of the police.

"I assume that you thought you were dealing with one blackmail demand, made upon my daughter. The way you handled it may or may not have been the wisest move to make under the circumstances. But, as you can see, the pattern is much more complex than you realized. I simply wanted you to understand that situation."

"Why not talk with your husband about this and tell him the whole story?" Mason asked.

"I may," she said, "later on."

"Do you know where your husband is now?"

"I think he's out at the lake but he is to join me here in town later on."

"And your daughter?"

"I don't know where she is, but she intends to spend the night at the lake residence. I am going to telephone her with some excuse and ask her to come into town and stay at our apartment here. Since my husband will be with me, I don't want her staying out there alone."

Mrs. Bancroft looked at her watch, said, "And I have a good many things to do. I'm going to have to hurry. Good afternoon, Mr. Mason."

She rose, very sure of herself, flashed an inclusive smile at both Mason and Della Street, and moved to the exit door.

"Thank you for seeing me," she said, and went out.

Mason and Della Street exchanged glances.

"So," Della Street said, "Harlow Bancroft was thinking about the wrong criminal record and the wrong set of fingerprints."

"Or was he?" Mason said. "Of course, that's a natural presumption, but we are dealing with a highly complex situation and *two* blackmailers."

Mason drummed with his fingertips on the edge of the desk.

The phone rang sharply.

Della Street answered it, said to Mason, "Harlow Bancroft on the line."

"Returning our call?" Mason asked.

"I don't know," she said. "Gertie says he's on the line."

Mason picked up the instrument, said, "Hello, Bancroft. I was trying to get in touch with you."

"So I understand," Bancroft said. "I wanted to see you but there isn't time for me to get in and talk with you."

"Where are you now?"

"At my summer home on the lake."

"You're going to stay there tonight?"

"I don't know just yet. However, that's neither here nor there. What I wanted to tell you was that I've been a heel. I've been selfish and— Well, forget all that I told you. That blackmailing business wasn't anything like what I thought it was. It's something else. . . . I will have to explain to you in person, but— We may be all mixed up on this thing. It may be something entirely different from what you think it is."

"It *may* be," Mason said dryly. "What do you want me to do?"

"Do whatever you think is best," Bancroft said.

"How did you find out about all this?"

"I had a heart-to-heart talk with my stepdaughter."

"Did you tell her what you told me?" Mason asked.

"I didn't," Bancroft said. "She was doing the talking. I— This isn't the time to tell my family anything, Mason. All I can do is to try and be of help. . . . Now look, you've had ideas about playing with blackmailers.

"If the blackmailers were striking at me, the situation would have been different, but as it is it's— Well, I can't tell you over the phone, but it's a collateral matter and I think the best thing to do may be to pay them off and gain time. I think that it is, after all, rather a petty matter—that is, comparatively petty—and . . . well, I'm afraid your tactics have been— Well, you may have been too rough. You may be rocking the boat."

"I told you I was going to rock the boat," Mason said.

"But you're rocking it pretty violently," Bancroft said, "and you may have got the wrong boat. . . . I want to see you tomorrow morning."

"Why not tonight?" Mason said. "If it's a matter of this importance I'll wait for you."

"No, I can't make it tonight. There are other things— Just sit tight, Mason, and I'll see you in the morning. Ten o'clock?"

"All right, at ten," Mason said. "Now what about that missing gun, Bancroft? Does your stepdaughter have it?"

"She says she doesn't. She seemed very much surprised when I asked her about it. My stepdaughter is in a very peculiar position. Newspapermen are trying their damnedest to find out all about this blackmail scheme, and some person, probably a newspaper reporter, tried to get Rosena to commit herself over the telephone but she told him off and slammed down the phone. However, it may have been one of the blackmailers. . . . I tell you, Mason, I think the best thing to do is to pay off.

"Now, I appreciate everything you've done, and of course I want you to hold what I told you in the strictest confidence, the most complete confidence. But just sit tight for a while and leave matters to us. I think we can handle them all right one way or another."

"I've told you," Mason said, "there are only four ways to handle a blackmailer."

"I know, I know, but one of the ways was to pay off and I have a very definite feeling that we're dealing with rather small potatoes, that there's no need to bring out our big artillery. I think the passage of time will take care of everything. All we're doing at the moment is buying time."

"I think I should see you tonight," Mason said.

"It's absolutely impossible. I've got other things. . . . But I'll see you tomorrow."

"At ten?" Mason asked.

"At ten. In the meantime, don't stir things up any more. Just take it easy and let the dust settle."

"Very well," Mason told him. "I'll sit tight, although I have several lines out that may hook a fish."

"No, no, no," Bancroft said. "We don't want to hook any fish at this time. We just want to sit tight and forget it. Just let everything go. It's only a question of money and I'm willing to pay. That's what I want to do."

"You're the doctor," Mason said. "I'll see you tomorrow."

Mason hung up, then called Paul Drake, said, "Paul, I want a bodyguard for Rosena Andrews. I want a man on the job with Eve Amory, just to insure her personal safety. Aside from that, we're pulling in our horns—at least for tonight."

"Okay," Drake said, "I've got the men, in case you want any more than that."

"No, that's enough," Mason told him. "And you're going to have to use the greatest discretion. We don't want anyone to even suspect a shadowing job, but keep me posted, Paul."

"Okay," Drake said cheerfully. "Can do and will do."

9

At nine-thirty that night the unlisted telephone in Mason's apartment rang, and Mason, knowing that only Della Street and Paul Drake had that telephone number, promptly picked up the instrument and said, "Yes?"

Paul Drake's voice came over the line. "I took some responsibility on my own initiative, Perry. I don't know whether I did the right thing or not."

"What happened?"

"I had a man on Eve Amory, as you suggested. A fellow who was keeping in the background but was a good rough, two-fisted guy, a little on the elderly side, but still able to give a good account of himself in a roughhouse.

"The point is, he'd been on the police force for twelve years, attached to the bunco squad, and had done some work on the blackmailing end of things. I felt he'd be a good man to—"

"All right, never mind the buildup," Mason said. "What happened?"

"Well, about seven-forty a fellow parked in front of Eve Amory's apartment house and from the way he was acting my man started giving him the once-over.

"This fellow went to a phone booth and put through a call, probably to Eve Amory, but of course my man had no way of knowing it at the time. But in about ten minutes Eve came walking out of the apartment house and this fellow drew up in his automobile, flashed her a signal, and she got in the car.

"My man tagged along behind, thinking it might be some sort of a snatch, but apparently it was just a conference because the fellow drove her around four or five blocks, then parked at the curb, talked with her for half an hour and then took her back to her apartment house and let her out."

"Any idea of what it was all about?" Mason asked.

"He was trying to get her to sign a paper, or at least that's the way it looked to my man. This fellow had a paper that he kept pushing in front of her. She'd hesitate for a while, act as though she was on the point of signing, then push the paper back. Then they'd talk for a while and then he'd push the paper over toward her again."

"Where was your man that he could see all this?"

"That's the worst of it," Drake said. "He couldn't see it all. There was no place where he could park behind them without making them suspicious so he had to drive past two or three times and once pretended that he was trying to get into a parking place. Actually there wasn't any parking place there. It was too small, but he manipulated his car around back and forth. They were so engrossed in what they were doing that they paid no attention to him.

"Anyway, what I'm coming to, Perry, is that when this man pulled out after leaving Eve Amory at her apartment house, my man played a hunch and started following this guy."

"He left Eve Amory unprotected?" Mason asked.

"No, he has a two-way radio in his car so he can keep in constant touch with me. He told me what was happening and told me to send another man down to cover Eve, that he felt he should tail this fellow. He thought there was something familiar about him in just the glimpses he'd had of him."

"Go ahead," Mason said.

"Well, anyway, my man tailed this fellow down to the Ajax-Delsey apartment house. Now, that's down toward the beach and it's a cheap apartment house. Actually it's nothing much more than a rooming house, but the point of it is that when this fellow got out of the car my man placed him"

"What do you mean, he placed him? Does he have a record?"

"That's right. He's Stilson L. Kelsey, known as Con-King Kelsey. He went in the rooming house and my man found out he had a room there. He radio-phoned in asking for instructions and I told him to sit on the rooming house for a while and see what happens. If Kelsey goes out I want him tagged."

"He found out that Kelsey has a room there?"

"That's right. He has a room there, and my man is sitting on the apartment house and keeping an eye on Kelsey's car, but if Kelsey does come out my man may not be able to keep him in sight."

"Why not?"

"A pea-soup fog which has settled in over the beach. It's clear toward town but if Kelsey should start the other way it's thicker than gravy."

"Have you heard anything from Eve Amory?" Mason asked.

"No, whatever the deal was, this guy put enough pressure on her so she hasn't reported. My man said it looked like she was almost ready to sign the paper. She was hesitating."

"But she didn't sign?"

"My man thinks she didn't."

"All right," Mason said. "Keep your tail on Kelsey."

"For how long?"

"Hell, all night, if necessary," Mason said.

"He'll have to have relief. He goes off duty at midnight."

"Then send a relief down to take over at midnight," Mason said. "Let's see what Kelsey does. I want to find out who's in on this.

"Also keep a good man on Eve Amory and see if she goes anywhere. I want to keep an eye on her. If this Kelsey fellow comes back and tries to put any more pressure on her, phone me no matter what hour it is. I want to get in on the act personally."

"Okay," Drake said. "You foot the bills, I'll run 'em up, Perry."

10

It was a highly nervous, excited Harlow Bancroft who kept his appointment the next morning.

The man seemed to be almost on the point of cracking up.

"What is it, Bancroft?" Mason asked.

"My wife," Bancroft said.

"What about her?"

"Mr. Mason, what I'm going to tell you has to be in absolute confidence."

"Certainly," Mason said. "It is. Anything you say is a privileged, professional communication."

"You said there were four ways of dealing with blackmailers," Bancroft said. "Do you remember the methods?"

"Yes."

"One of the ways," Bancroft said, "was to kill the blackmailer." Mason's eyes narrowed. "You mean your wife has done that?"

"Yes."

"When?"

"Last night."

"Where?"

"Aboard my yacht, the *Jinesa*."

"Who knows about it?" Mason asked. "Did you report it to the police?"

"No. I'm afraid that's where we've made our big mistake."

"Better tell me about it," Mason said, "and tell me about it fast."

Bancroft said, "My wife had some charitable bazaar work that she was going to do the first part of the evening last night and then she wanted me to join her at our apartment, saying that she might be late getting in, on account of her other commitments.

"Now, apparently what actually happened was this. . . . Now, Mason, you've *got* to assure me this will be absolutely confidential."

"Keep talking," Mason said. "You may not have much time."

"Well, it seems that Jetson Blair had a brother, Carleton Rasmus Blair, who was supposed to have been dead—"

"I know all about that," Mason interrupted.

"All right. Carleton Blair was living at the Ajax-Delsey Apartments under the name of Irwin Victor Fordyce. He had a very close friend by the name of Willmer Gilly, who was also living there. The place has rather a low reputation. Apparently crooks know about it as a good place to hole up where the landlord doesn't ask too many questions and isn't at all curious.

"Gilly had been released from San Quentin at about the same time Fordyce had and the two were inseparable; that is, Fordyce thought that Gilly was his great friend.

"So Fordyce, reading in the paper all about the society gossip connecting Jetson Blair and Rosena Andrews, finally confided to Gilly that he was a member of the Blair family, that he was the black sheep of the family and everyone thought he was dead.

"Apparently Gilly decided to cash in on the information. He put the bite on Rosena and he put the bite on Phyllis, my wife, and Phyllis paid off."

"Go ahead," Mason said.

"Then, after all this publicity in connection with the money in the coffee can, Gilly tried to get Rosena to make another payment. Rosena was smart enough to pretend she thought she was talking with some newspaper reporter and refused to commit herself.

"So Gilly apparently decided to go to Phyllis personally.

"Now, here comes the thing I can't understand. Phyllis decided that since Irwin Fordyce was the club the blackmailers were using, she should go and find out exactly what Fordyce knew about all this.

"So she found out where Fordyce was, at the Ajax-Delsey Apartments, went there and put it up to him, asking him whether he was a blackmailer and a heel as well as being the black sheep of the family.

"Fordyce was completely flabbergasted to think that Gilly would have tried anything like that. He swore he would kill Gilly. Then he calmed down somewhat and told Phyllis that he'd take care of it, to pay no more attention to any blackmail demands.

"Phyllis became alarmed.

"Phyllis also knew, from what Gilly had said, that the police might be looking for Fordyce in connection with a service-station holdup and she was afraid of what would happen if Fordyce got together with Gilly. She was afraid the fat might *really* be in the fire, so she suggested to Fordyce that he come with her, that she would drive him down to our yacht, the *Jinesa,* then get him some money, and he could spend a week or two on the yacht, which would be the last place anyone would look for him.

"Now, of course, Phyllis had no right to do that, particularly as she knew that Fordyce was wanted by the police."

"How did she know it?" Mason asked.

"Gilly had told her."

"The word of a blackmailer," Mason said. "That's nothing."

"I'm glad to hear you say so because that part of it bothered me."

"All right. Let's get down to Gilly. What about him?"

"Well, Phyllis took Fordyce down to the yacht, put him aboard the yacht, told him to stay there. Then she took the dinghy, rowed back to the yacht club, got in her car, went to some friends whom she knew she could trust and whom she knew always kept quite a bit of cash on hand because they quite frequently took off for Las Vegas to gamble. She got those people to cash her check for three thousand dollars in fifties and hundreds.

"Then she returned to the boat, intending to give the money to Fordyce, but when she got aboard the boat she found to her consternation that Fordyce had disappeared and Gilly was aboard the boat."

"What had happened to Fordyce?" Mason asked.

"Probably," Bancroft said, "he was murdered, because Gilly was the only one aboard the boat and Gilly's attitude was decidedly threatening."

"And what happened?"

"Phyllis had this gun in her purse and the three thousand dollars. She started stalling for time. Now, there's quite a long story here. When she first came aboard she saw this shadowy figure up in the bow of the boat, raising the anchor. She thought it was Fordyce."

"The boat was not on a mooring?"

"Not at the time. It was on an anchor because the mooring was undergoing repair."

"All right," Mason said, "go on."

"This figure heard her come aboard and made a half-hitch around the bitt in the bow with the anchor chain, then came on back to the main cabin. Now, the point is the engine had been started and the boat was underway at that time. A thick fog was coming in and within a matter of seconds the boat was enveloped in this blanket of fog."

"Why was the boat underway?" Mason asked.

"Apparently so that whatever happened would be masked by this fog. Gilly had definite plans and he evidently was planning to beach the boat and then leave it so Phyllis would be blamed for the disappearance of Fordyce."

"Go ahead," Mason said.

"Well, Gilly accused Phyllis of double-crossing him and Phyllis wanted to know what had happened to Fordyce, and one thing led to another and Gilly told her that he knew she'd gone to get some money and he wanted that money. She told him she wasn't going to give it to him and Gilly became threatening. He said out in this fog he could weight her body and throw her overboard.

"That was when Phyllis pulled the gun out of the purse and told him to put his hands up.

"She thought, of course, that as soon as she pointed a gun at him and told him to put his hands up, he'd wilt. Instead of that he cursed and started for her."

"And then?" Mason asked.

"Remember," Bancroft said, "the anchor was dragging. That is, there was about fiffiteen or twenty feet of chain out—somewhere along there, I guess, and at that moment the anchor hit something, either a submerged log or a rock or a piece of hard ground, and Phyllis was thrown off balance and involuntarily her finger tightened on the trigger. She shot Gilly at point-blank range and he went down like a log."

"What did your wife do?"

"She was in a panic. She dashed to the side of the boat and jumped overboard."

"The gun?" Mason asked.

"She thinks she had the gun and the purse in her hand when she went overboard, but overboard she went and started swimming toward the shore. She dropped the gun. Her purse slipped off her wrist."

"It was thick fog. Could she see the shore?"

"She could see the dim aura of lights, and as it turned out it was only a few feet to a place where the water was shallow enough so she could wade. She waded out of the water and found she was right near one of the fueling wharves where we get gas for the boat. That was only a few hundred feet from the yacht club parking space, so she just kept on running in her wet clothes, got to the parking lot, jumped in her car and drove to the apartment."

"Leaving the boat right there?"

"Right there."

"With the body in it?"

"Yes."

"How does she know he was dead?"

"She felt sure he was from the way he fell and the fact that she shot him at point-blank range, right in the chest."

"And that was Gilly?"

"That was Gilly."

"And she doesn't know what happened to Fordyce?"

"No."

Mason said, "All right, this thing begins to check into a pattern. Fordyce confided in Gilly. Gilly has a friend, a very expert blackmailer and confidence man known as Con-King Kelsey. . . . Now, what about the yacht?"

"That's the point," Bancroft said. "As soon as it was daylight I drove down to the yacht, and the yacht isn't there."

"It isn't there?" Mason repeated.

Bancroft shook his head. "You see, when this happened last night the tide was low. The tide had just turned and was starting to come in. So apparently during the night the tide came in enough so the boat floated and drifted back out into the harbor and then ran aground someplace at high tide."

"When did your wife tell you this?"

"About ten o'clock last night."

"Why didn't you call me or the police?"

"I didn't dare call the police and I felt I'd better wait until this morning to see you. I didn't know where I could reach you except through the Drake Detective Agency, and— Well, hell's bells, Mason, my wife was absolutely hysterical. If she'd called the police in that condition she'd have gone all to pieces. That would have

meant the newspapers would have had the whole story of Fordyce. . . . Damn it, it wasn't murder. It was self-defense. I took it
on myself to assume the responsibility. We'll let the police come to
us."

"All right. That's a hell of a way to play it, however. It could
have been self-defense if she'd gone to the police. It can be murder
by the time the police go to you."

"Well, I had a decision to make and I made it. I put my wife
under heavy sedation with some drugs I had in the apartment."

"But don't you realize," Mason said, "that all of this blackmail
story is going to come out anyway? This is a murder."

"I know it will eventually, but that's why I'm telling you now and
putting things in your hands. You've got to adopt the attitude that
Phyllis can't tell her story now without disclosing a blackmail plot
we can't afford to have become public property, and therefore she
refuses to make any statement at all.

"We're playing for time. We *have* to play it that way."

"We do now," Mason said grimly. "Last night we could have had
an option. We have none now. It isn't going to do any good to go
to the police at this late date and tell our story. We're hooked now.
And we've got to find out more about the facts. The first thing to do
is to find that yacht."

"There's still a thick fog over the bay."

"We'll get a helicopter," Mason said, "and sit on top of it until
it lifts."

The lawyer turned to Della Street. "Ring up our airport service.
Tell them we want to charter a four-place helicopter as of now."

The lawyer reached for his hat. "Come on, Bancroft, let's go."

The phone rang as Mason was halfway to the door. Della
glanced inquiringly at the lawyer, received his nod and moved
back to pick up the receiver. "Yes, Gertie," she said. "What is it?"

She motioned to Perry Mason, said, "Eve Amory is calling."

Mason frowned, turned back to the telephone on his desk, picked
up the receiver, said, "I'll talk with her. Put her on."

A moment later when he had Eve Amory on the line he said,
"Yes, Eve. This is Perry Mason. What seems to be the trouble?"

She said, "I'm going to have to chicken out on you, Mr. Mason."

"What do you mean?"

"I mean," she said, "that I'm signing a statement that this whole thing was a publicity stunt, that the money was put up by a friend of mine, an angel, and we concocted the blackmail note and arranged for me to find the money and get publicity that way, that the whole thing was a scheme for publicity."

"You can't do that, Eve," Mason said. "That isn't the truth and you know it."

"But if I sign that statement," she said, "I can get out from under."

"From under what?"

"Things that . . . well, pressures."

"You aren't going to get out from under any pressures that way," Mason said.

"They tell me I am."

"Who tells you?"

"Well . . . people."

"Did they leave a statement with you for you to sign?" Mason asked.

"Yes."

Mason said, "I want you to do something, Eve. I want you to come up to my office and talk with me before you sign that statement."

"They've given me a deadline of two o'clock this afternoon."

"All right," Mason said, "tell whoever it was that you're going to be at my office at two o'clock this afternoon and you'll sign the statement then."

"I don't think these people will come to your office."

"Then tell them they can't get the statement. Tell them you're willing but you have to get a clearance with me."

"I don't think that would work. They wouldn't—"

"Well, try it," Mason said. "Will you do that much?"

"I'll try, yes."

"Promise?"

"I promise."

"Okay," Mason said, and hung up the telephone.

"These damned blackmailers," Mason said to Bancroft, "certainly get around. If a man is clever enough and ruthless enough and has enough sources of information— Oh well, let's go."

11

The day was warm and sunny inland but a thick bank of white clouds stayed motionless in the west.

The helicopter pilot, moving at about five hundred feet above the ground, said to Mason, "I don't like the looks of it, Mr. Mason. We can skirt along the edges but I doubt very much if we can see anything."

"You can fly low?" Mason asked.

"Sure, I can fly low. I can fly five feet over the water as far as that's concerned, but I'm not going to go messing around there in a fog at low elevation without knowing what I'm getting into."

"Do the best you can," Mason said.

"Sometimes the action of the helicopter clears fog up quite rapidly," the pilot said. "We churn up a lot of air and if we can get on the boundary between the clear air and the fog we may be able to get enough agitation to start things clearing. Sometimes it works and sometimes it doesn't."

"Well, let's try it," Mason said.

The helicopter moved at a steady seventy-five knots an hour, moving toward the white bank of clouds which seemed to grow higher and thicker as the machine approached them.

"I'm afraid it's no go," the pilot said. "We can hang around on the edges of the fog and survey the situation but this isn't going to do you much good. It's a thick, pea-soup fog and it's hanging on all day, apparently."

"Can you get down right along the ground and see how far you can go?"

"I'll try it but as soon as I lose visibility I'm going to backtrack."

"Well, sometimes it's lighter right along the water," Mason said. "Let's try it."

The pilot lowered the helicopter until they were flying over fields at housetop level. Then the first tendrils of fog enveloped them. The action of the rotor on the helicopter caused the fog particles to swirl and for a moment the fog right around the machine seemed to lift. Then it settled down again and the pilot suddenly turned the machine, came back up and out.

"Nothing doing," he said. "I'm sorry, but I'm not going into that stuff. This is the thickest I've ever seen it at this time of the day. There's not a breath of air stirring. This is just like flying in milk."

"We can get above it?" Mason asked.

"Sure, we can get above it but that won't do you any good. You'll be looking down on a solid white carpet."

"Okay," Mason said, "let's go back. Hold yourself in readiness. As soon as the fog starts to lift I want to make a survey of the harbor."

Mason turned to Bancroft. "It's the best we can do, Bancroft," he said. "I don't know of any other way."

"Nor do I," Bancroft said.

Mason said, "I'm going to want to talk with your wife."

Bancroft nodded. "She's still under sedation," he said. "I took it on myself to do that on my own responsibility. I gave her a heavy dose of sleeping pills. You can imagine she was—"

Mason gave a meaning glance at the pilot of the helicopter and Bancroft lapsed into silence.

Mason said to the pilot, "I want you to keep this thing chartered on an hourly basis all day. Just as soon as the fog lifts so we can get in over the harbor I want to go in. Do you understand?"

"I understand perfectly."

"Call me the minute it starts to break," Mason said.

"I'll do it but it may not break all day, Mr. Mason, having hung on this late."

"You just sit there and wait," Mason said. "If it breaks, we'll go. Now, there's a downtown heliport where you can be waiting?"

"Within a few minutes of your office," the pilot said.

"Sit tight," Mason told him, "and keep in touch with conditions at the harbor. Phone me the minute there's any chance of getting in there."

The pilot nodded and Mason was silent until the helicopter had landed.

Driving back to his office, Mason said to Bancroft, "Now, *you* know the yacht *wasn't* at the place where your wife said she jumped overboard?"

"Yes."

"How do you know that?"

"Because I drove down there."

"There was a heavy fog?"

"That's right, but I was able to drive along in the fog—just creeping along with my lights on and my windshield wiper going."

"But your wife described the place?"

"Perfectly."

"And you looked there?"

"Yes. I walked out on the fueling wharf early this morning."

"And the boat wasn't there?"

"No."

"You're sure?"

"Yes."

Mason said, "You should have gone to the police just as soon as your wife told her story."

"I know, but I told you why I couldn't afford to do it," Bancroft said. "That was a chance I couldn't take."

"As I understand it," Mason said, "the gun went off accidentally."

"Phyllis was holding it, pointing it at this man and warning him and—"

"The gun went off accidentally," Mason interrupted.

"Well, of course she—"

"The gun went off accidentally," Mason interposed. "The yacht ran aground."

"Not the yacht, the dragging anchor hooked on something and . . . well, there was a jar and the yacht swung around a bit."

"And the gun went off accidentally."

Bancroft thought that over a few moments, then said, "Yes. The gun went off accidentally."

"And this man, this blackmailer, what was his name? Gillis?"

"Gilly," Bancroft said.

"All right, Gilly flung up his hands and pitched forward on his face."

"Yes."

"Your wife dropped everything, ran to the rail and jumped overboard."

"She dropped things after she jumped; that is, she thinks she did. She has a dim recollection of her purse slidding off her arm just as she jumped for the water."

"She was frightened," Mason said.

"Yes."

"In fear of her life."

"Yes, of course."

"Hysterical," Mason said. "A blackmailer had threatened her with death and she thought he was going to come rushing to the rail and start shooting at her."

"Well . . . of course he had been struck by the bullet and—"

"She doesn't *know* where the bullet struck," Mason said. "It might have hit him in the shoulder, it might have hit him in the chest, but she was frightened. She thought he was going to run to the rail and start shooting."

"Well . . . yes, I guess so."

"Don't guess," Mason said. "It fits in with her actions and you've got to have a story that fits in with her actions."

Bancroft thought that over for a moment, then slowly nodded.

Mason said, "I've got an important appointment at my office—one I can't afford to miss. I want you to be waiting in readiness. Either you'll have to hang around my office or be where I can reach you by telephone at a moment's notice."

"Why is it so important to locate the yacht?" Bancroft said.

"Because I want to get a look at it before the police do, if possible," Mason said.

"Of course we have no idea where the yacht wound up," Bancroft pointed out.

"Exactly," Mason told him. "Your wife found Gilly hoisting the anchor, hand over hand. When he saw her, he made a half-hitch around the bitt with the anchor chain and came back to meet her."

Bancroft nodded.

"The motor was running?" Mason asked.

"That's right."

"He threw the clutch in?"

"That's right."

"There's a control on the front deck so he could do that?"

"Yes, it's a special control, made so that one man can pull up the anchor and then get headway just as soon as the anchor is up.

Sometimes I sail it all by myself and I had that forward control put in."

"What time did the shooting take place?" Mason asked.

"Somewhere around eight-thirty to nine."

"Where were *you* at that time?"

"Waiting for my wife."

"Anybody know where you were?"

"No."

Mason regarded Bancroft thoughtfully. "Of course, Bancroft," he said, "if it should turn out the killing was with *your* gun on *your* yacht, the police *could* decide that you had been trying to protect your wife and had taken things into your own hands."

Bancroft showed surprise. "You mean that they could claim I . . . ?"

"Exactly," Mason said. "Your story of giving your wife heavy sedation and not letting her go to the police—"

"Why, I was trying to protect her from questioning when she was emotionally upset, and—"

"And trying to keep the thing out of the newspapers," Mason said.

"Well, yes."

"You've gained a little time," Mason said, "but by the time it breaks it's going to be one hell of a story."

12

A little before two o'clock Mason's unlisted phone rang sharply.

Mason scooped up the instrument, said, "Yes, Paul. What is it?"

Paul Drake's voice came crisply over the wire. "Just received a call from the man who is staked out on Eve Amory's apartment. A man answering the description of Con-King Kelsey just pulled up in a car and went in."

"Alone?" Mason asked.

"Alone," Drake said.

"Your man has a phone in his car?"

"That's right. He can keep in touch at all times."

"Okay," Mason said. "I'm going out there, Paul."

"Want company?" Drake asked.

"I think I can handle it alone," Mason said. "A witness might be a little unhandy. Now, I'm sitting on a deal down at the harbor. We're waiting for the fog to lift. I understand it may lift any time and I have a helicopter standing by. If Della Street phones that the fog is lifting, get your man who's staked out on the Amory apartment to come in and tip me off."

Mason slammed down the receiver, said to Della, "Keep on the job, Della. The minute that fog starts to lift I want to get down to look for that yacht."

"You're going out to see Kelsey?" she asked.

"I'm going to have a talk with a blackmailer," Mason said. "A perfectly frank, heart-to-heart talk."

"You be careful," she warned.

Mason grinned at her as he shot through the door.

Mason made time to Eve Amory's apartment house. Drake's man, who was staked out on the job, recognizing Mason, came forward and said, "He's still up there, Mr. Mason. You want me to go with you?"

"No, you stay here," Mason said. "You have radio communication in your car?"

"That's right."

"Keep in touch with the office," Mason said. "If they want me, come and get me."

"What'll I say?" the operative asked.

"Just that my office wants me," Mason said.

"How long will you be up there?"

"Not very long," Mason said.

He took the elevator, walked down the corridor and jabbed the mother-of-pearl call button on Eve Amory's apartment.

Chimes sounded on the inside.

After a moment Eve Amory opened the door.

"Hello," Mason said.

As she stood uncertainly in the doorway, Mason pushed on past her and entered the apartment, where a powerfully built man of around fifty years of age with steady, cold gray eyes looked up at him in venomous appraisal.

"And," Mason said, "I suppose you're Stilson L. Kelsey, sometimes referred to as Con-King Kelsey, and that document you're holding in your hand is something you're trying to get Eve Amory to sign.

"I'm here to tell you that she's not going to sign it, that I don't like blackmailers, and that you can get the hell out of here and leave this young woman alone or you're going to go to prison."

Kelsey slowly rose, pushed back the chair, said, "I don't like lawyers. I'm not a blackmailer. I'm a businessman. Call me a sharpshooter, if you want to. I'm smart enough to know a phoney setup when I see it.

"This wasn't blackmail, this was a publicity deal. It's as phoney as a three-dollar bill. For your information, Mr. Mason, Eve Amory has just admitted as much to me and I have in my hands a document showing that the whole thing was a frame-up."

"I'll show you the kind of a frame-up it was," Mason said. "Who do you think put that three thousand dollars in the coffee can?"

"I don't know and I don't give a damn."

"I can show exactly who put it in, and that it wasn't any publicity stunt," Mason said.

Kelsey regarded the lawyer with shrewd, unblinking eyes, sizing up the situation.

"All right," he said at length, "I'll put my cards on the table with you, Mister Lawyer. I get around. I know people. I know a guy by the name of Willmer Gilly. Gilly uncovered some information and started putting the bite on certain people I won't name at the moment.

"I'm in a position to control Gilly. If somebody wants to deal with me, okay. If they don't, okay."

"They don't," Mason said. "Get out."

"Are you paying the rent on this apartment?" Kelsey asked.

"I'm a taxpayer," Mason said. "I'm paying part of the cost of maintaining the city jail. Now then, I'm going to call your bluff, Kelsey, and I'm going to call it cold. You try to bring any pressure to bear on this young woman to state that this was a publicity stunt, and I'll come out and show that I put up the money that went in that coffee can. I'll have the canceled check to prove it and the statement of the banker that the money was handed over to me in ten- and twenty-dollar bills and some of the numbers of the bills were kept on a list just to prove where the money came from, in case the question ever arose. Eve Amory isn't going to sign this statement saying that it was a publicity stunt and that you put up the money or had anything to do with putting up the money because that's false, and if you try to make any commotion about it we'll have you up for extortion, for obtaining money under false pretenses, and making false statements to the authorities."

With that, Mason stepped forward, picked up the paper that was on the table in front of Kelsey, tore it into four pieces, and tossed the pieces to the floor.

"Got anything to say, Kelsey?" he asked.

Kelsey regarded him with cold fury. "Not now," he said. "I'll have something to say later."

"Say it to me," Mason said.

"I'll say it to you," Kelsey said, "and when you hear it, you won't like it."

Chimes sounded on the door.

Mason jerked it open. Drake's man was standing on the threshold. "Your office phoned. They want you," he said.

Mason jerked his head toward the door and said to Kelsey, "Out."

"You don't own this apartment," Kelsey said.

"That's right," Mason told him. "Out."

"You can't put me out."

"Want to bet?"

"Now that reinforcements have arrived, maybe you can," Kelsey said. "Who the hell is this guy?"

"Private detective," Mason said. "He's had you under surveillance. We're getting evidence to throw the book at you on extortion."

Kelsey's eyes wavered. He looked for a moment like a trapped animal.

"Show him your credentials," Mason said to the operative.

The operative took a leather folder from his pocket, exhibited his credentials.

"All right," Kelsey said, "all right, I'll go. But you haven't got a case against me. You may have something against Gilly but you haven't got it against me."

Mason said, "Want to bet?"

"No, I don't want to bet," Kelsey flared at him. "I've half a mind to—"

"Go ahead," Mason said, as Kelsey's voice trailed off into silence.

Kelsey turned, stalked out of the apartment.

Mason said to Eve Amory, "Come on, Eve. You're going to Paul Drake's office. You're going to stay there for a few hours until we get this thing ironed out."

"He threatened to—"

"Sure he did," Mason said. "He makes his living by making threats. His threats are bluffs. He isn't going to do any of the things he said he was going to do. He can only get by, by frightening people. Come on, you're going to Drake's office and sit there for a while. Get your things. I'm in a hurry."

"It'll take me a few minutes," she said. "I—"

"All right," Mason said, "I can't wait."

He turned to Drake's operative. "Put her in your car," he said. "Drive her up to Drake's office. Let her stay there for a couple of hours. If that man, Kelsey, should be waiting outside and try to make trouble—do you think you can handle him?"

"With one hand," the operative said with calm confidence.

"All right," Mason said, "handle him."

The lawyer turned, dashed down the corridor, took the stairs two at a time, jumped in his car and hurried to the heliport.

Bancroft and Della Street were waiting for him.

"Been here long?" Mason asked.

"Just a few minutes," Bancroft said. "The pilot said the fog is lifting down at the bay."

"Let's go," Mason told him.

They strapped themselves in the helicopter, and the pilot revved the engine and abruptly took off. They gained elevation rapidly, skimming over the city and the outskirts, then came down lower and raced along over relatively open country.

The fog bank was still ahead of them but as they approached the bay the fog was melting into wisps and streamers, and the pilot, carefully skirting the edge of the fog, slowed the helicopter so that it was hovering motionless over the bay.

"All right," Bancroft shouted, "there's the yacht club over there. There's the mooring that the *Jinesa* usually occupies."

"Now show me the oil and gasoline wharf which was recognized last night," Mason said.

"A little over to the right," Bancroft told the pilot.

The helicopter hovered over the water.

"Right down here," Bancroft said.

"No sign of a boat here," Mason said. "Was there any wind last night?"

"No wind. It was dead calm. That's the reason a fog came in and stayed so long. There hasn't been any wind. It's just beginning to clear off with a slight land breeze."

Mason said, "The tide was coming in last night. Keep working up to the head of the bay."

The pilot obediently kept the helicopter moving slowly up the bay.

"Look! Look ahead!" Bancroft said suddenly. "That looks like her."

"Where?"

"About a mile up ahead."

Mason nodded to the pilot who sent the helicopter into more rapid forward motion, eventually hovering over a yacht which was anchored out by the edge of the shore line along some mud and sand flats at the head of the bay.

"That your boat?" Mason asked.

Bancroft nodded.

"It seems to be anchored," Mason said.

"That's right."

"The tide is now running out?"

"Right."

"And the anchor is holding it."

"Yes."

"Any idea about how deep the water is here?"

"Judging from what I know of the bay and the angle of the anchor chain, I'd say the water was ten or twelve feet deep and there's about twenty or twenty-five feet of anchor chain out."

Mason said, "Notice that the dinghy is still attached to the boat."

"I've noticed that," Bancroft said.

Mason said, "Evidently the boat has been stolen. I think we'd better have a representative of the sheriff's office with us when we go aboard."

The helicopter pilot said, "There's a sheriff's substation up here a little ways. I can land the helicopter there if you want. Also I have an aerial camera set up in this crate. I can take pictures if you want."

"We want," Mason said. "Both the sheriff and the pictures, but don't say anything about the pictures for a while."

A few moments later the helicopter settled to a landing by a sheriff's substation.

Mason quickly explained to the deputy, "We have reason to believe that Mr. Bancroft's yacht was stolen last night. We've been looking for it and finally found it. It's riding at anchor out here and whoever stole it is probably still aboard because the dinghy is still tied to it. Want to look?"

"We'll look," the deputy said.

"Got a boat?"

"We have a boat."

"Let's go," Mason told him.

"I'll stay with the helicopter until you get back," the pilot said.

The deputy drove them to a landing where they boarded a speedboat and started up the bay.

"Just keep going," Mason said. "We'll tell you when you're coming to it."

"It's about four miles up here near the sand flats," Bancroft said.

"At anchor?"

"At anchor."

They moved at high speed up the channel, then slowed as they got into shallower water.

"This is your boat ahead?" the deputy asked.

"That's it," Bancroft said.

The deputy piloted the yacht around the boat. "Ahoy the *Jinesa!*" he called. "Anyone aboard?"

There was no answer.

The deputy said, "I'm going aboard and take a look."

"Want us with you?" Mason asked.

The deputy shook his head. "You'd better wait here. You say the boat was stolen?"

Bancroft made no answer.

The deputy maneuvered the speedboat up to the side of the *Jinesa,* put over a couple of rubber bumpers and tied the two boats together, then sprang aboard lightly.

Bancroft said in a low voice to Mason, "Mason, I'm going to take the rap."

"What do you mean?"

"If Gilly is dead I'm going to say that I shot him and—"

"You keep your mouth shut," Mason said. "The best that we can do now is to rely on the fact that the state has to prove a case against a defendant beyond all reasonable doubt.

"Now, you can take this much responsibility. You can state that your wife was hysterical, that you gave her a strong sedative and insisted that she take enough so that it completely put her out.

"But remember this. They can't find the gun that did the shooting because your wife dropped the gun overboard when she jumped."

"But can't they find where she jumped and send down a diver and pick up the gun? It's in shallow water on a smooth bottom."

"She doesn't need to tell her story," Mason said. "She's gone this far without it and she's got to sit tight now. This isn't the way I like to handle a case, but we're in a spot where it's the only way we can handle the case. If and when the time comes for your wife to tell her story, we'll tell it. But remember that your wife boarded the yacht with a man by the name of Irwin Fordyce. The police find the yacht with Fordyce gone and Gilly killed. They're not going to make any charges until they find Fordyce and get his story."

"And when they get his story?" Bancroft asked.

"When they get his story," Mason said, "the case may be mixed up all to hell. Your wife has simply got to adopt the position that there are reasons why she can't tell everything that happened. She is going to have to sit tight as to certain phases of what happened last night. She'll state that she'll tell her story at the proper time, but that there are reasons why she doesn't want to make a public statement at this time."

"That's going to look like hell," Bancroft said.

"You got any suggestions that will keep it from looking like hell?" Mason asked. "What you should have done was to have called me last night and let me tell her story to the police about how she had been attacked and had fired wildly in self-defense, not knowing whether she had hit her assailant or not."

"She knows she hit him," Bancroft said. "He fell forward and was motionless. Evidently the bullet killed him instantly. She—"

The deputy came back on deck and said, "Look here, we've got a complicated situation. There's a dead man aboard. He's been dead for some time. Apparently he's been shot through the heart."

"That," Mason said, "complicates the situation."

The deputy looked at him soberly. "That," he said, "is the understatement of the month, and I am now beginning to wonder just why it happened that a yacht owner reporting a stolen boat has one of the leading criminal attorneys in the state along with him."

Mason grinned and said, "That's a long story, my friend."

"Do you want to start telling it now?" the deputy asked.

"No," Mason said.

"We can get the facts," the deputy said. "We can get them the easy way or we can get them the hard way."

"How long has this man been dead?" Mason asked.

"Quite a while, apparently. I don't want to disturb things. I'm going to notify the sheriff, take this boat in charge, then we'll move it over to a wharf where we can get technical assistance in order to evaluate the evidence—and I warn both of you that anything you say may be used against you."

"You're going to move this boat?" Mason asked.

"We'll have to move it," the deputy said. "We have to get to a point where we can have fingerprint men, photographers and experts take a look at the body while it's still just the way we found it."

Mason started to say something, then checked himself.

"You're in charge here," he said.

"Want to make any statement?" the deputy asked.

Mason shook his head.

"Do you?" the deputy asked Bancroft.

"We'll wait until after the evidence has been evaluated," Mason said. "This comes as a distinct shock to us."

"Well," the deputy said, "you seem to have been pretty well prepared for the shock."

13

It was six o'clock before the sheriff's office released Bancroft and Mason. Della Street had been released within a few minutes after the boats had docked.

Driving back in Bancroft's car, the millionaire gave voice to his doubts.

"Do you suppose they've questioned my wife already?" he asked.

Mason said, "Why do you suppose they kept us in custody all this time? Of course they've questioned your wife, and your stepdaughter and any of the servants they could get hold of."

"I told my wife to say absolutely nothing, to say that she would make no statement unless I was present."

"And when you're present, what are you going to do?"

"Tell her to say nothing until you instruct her to," Bancroft said.

Mason said, "You should have called me last night, but you've taken the responsibility of advising her and all I can do is to take the situation as I find it and try to make the best I can out of it.

"Right now I'm not satisfied as to what did happen."

"What do you mean?"

Mason said, "I don't think you've told me all the story."

Bancroft sat quiet for a few minutes, then said, "All right, Mason, you'll just have to play it blind. It's up to the prosecution to prove their case against any defendant. They can't *prove* a case against my wife, and I don't think they can *prove* a case against me. I want you to act on the assumption that we can't either one of us afford to make a statement as to what happened last night and that it's up to the police to make a case."

"Sometimes," Mason said, "the police are pretty damned skillful."

"I know, but they can't actually prove anything—not with the evidence they have at hand, and of course as soon as they get Gilly's fingerprints they'll find out that he's an ex-convict and presumably a blackmailer."

"And then they'll tie his death up with the blackmail note that was found in the coffee can," Mason said, "and then what?"

"Then," Bancroft said, "they have a dead blackmailer and a woman who was presumably the victim of the blackmailer, but they can't prove my wife ever had any personal contact with Gilly and they can't prove I ever had any personal contact with Gilly."

"Let's hope so," Mason said.

"Usually," Bancroft said, "when a person is innocent he tells his story fairly and frankly to the police. Sometimes they believe him and sometimes they don't. If he's guilty he sits tight and doesn't say anything and leaves it up to the police to produce every bit of evidence they need to obtain a conviction."

"And so?" Mason asked.

"So," Bancroft said, "there's no reason why an innocent person can't take advantage of some of the loopholes that are open to a guilty person. In this case we're going to sit tight and let the police move forward step by step, counting on the fact that they'll stumble before they reach their goal."

Mason said, "You have left me no alternative. If you had called me last night when your wife returned to the apartment we could have told a story of self-defense that would have been convincing. It's too late to tell it now unless we first adopt the position that your wife's lips are sealed because she's trying to protect others. That's the attitude we're going to have to adopt."

"Go ahead and adopt it," Bancroft said.

Mason suddenly said, "All right, I'll adopt it on one condition."

"What's that?"

"That you tell me what *really* happened last night."

"I've told you."

"No, you haven't," Mason said. "You're passing up something. You're concealing something. I want the truth."

"You might not represent us if you knew the truth."

"A person is always entitled to a defense in court," Mason said, "no matter what the circumstances. I want to know the real facts."

"All right," Bancroft said, "I guess you suspect them anyway. My wife came home. She was soaking wet. She had plunged overboard with her clothes on. She told me the story.

"She had decided to let Irwin Fordyce have our yacht. She felt no one would look for him there. She felt that would get him out of circulation until after the wedding, and perhaps until after things blew over.

"Fordyce had had some yachting experience. She picked him up at his apartment, drove him down to the boat, put him aboard the boat, went to get some money for him, and returned to the boat.

"Now, there were lots of provisions on the boat. We always keep it well stocked with canned goods. He could have gone over to Catalina or down to Ensenada and lived the life of a yachtsman almost indefinitely."

"Go ahead," Mason said. "Tell me what happened."

"After my wife got the money and went back to the boat, there was no sign of Fordyce. Gilly was there. Gilly quite evidently intended to kill her. She pulled the gun on him, thinking that he would put up his hands and leave her in control of the situation.

"Instead of that he lunged toward her and at that instant the boat ran aground. My wife involuntarily pulled the trigger. Gilly fell dead at her feet. My wife jumped overboard, waded ashore, got the car and came to our apartment.

"She told me what had happened.

"Now, there's where I made my mistake. She was almost hysterical. I had a powerful narcotic that had been left with me in case of pain in connection with some gall bladder trouble I had been having. I gave her enough of that narcotic to put her into a deep sleep. I told her we'd tell her story to the police the next day when she felt more like it."

"And what did you do?" Mason asked.

Bancroft said, "All right, Mason, I'll tell you the truth. I drove down to the harbor."

"And got aboard the boat?"

"Mason, so help me, the boat wasn't in the position where it had been when she left it."

"What did you intend to do?"

"I intended to get the body of Gilly off the boat, take it out into the ocean, weight it with an anchor and drop it overboard. Then I intended to say nothing about it. No one could connect my wife with Gilly. No one could connect Gilly with my wife. No one could connect Gilly with me."

"And you couldn't find the boat?" Mason asked.

"The boat was gone. Remember, the tide was coming in. It was in and floated the boat and the current had taken it up the bay, but I couldn't find it because a thick fog had settled in and I was absolutely helpless. I prowled around the water front for two or three hours and then finally came home, completely licked."

"All right," Mason said, "I'm glad you've told me the truth finally. By your actions you burned your bridges. Your wife could have told a story of self-defense that would have been convincing if she had gone at once to the police."

"Can't she still tell it? She didn't know what I had in mind."

"The hell she didn't," Mason said grimly. "Don't try to tell *me* that."

"All right," Bancroft said, "I *did* tell her what I had in mind, and I told her to keep her mouth shut—no matter what happened to say nothing to anyone."

"Let's hope she follows that advice," Mason said. "There is a time and a place where she can tell her story, but in the meantime we've got to play this blackmail angle for all it's worth and let it appear that your wife is sacrificing herself and her own best interests for the purpose of protecting someone else.

"Now then, go on home. You'll find that while they were detaining us, the police have had a search warrant issued for your apartment, that they've gone through the place in search of— What's the matter?"

"Good heavens!" Bancroft said. "My wife's clothes, soaked with salt water. . . .She left them in the closet. I didn't have presence of mind enough to get rid of them."

"And your wife," Mason said, "what will she tell them?"

"She'll tell them nothing," Bancroft said. "I made her promise that before I left, that if anything happened and the police came she was to say absolutely nothing."

"That's going to be hard to do," Mason said.

"Don't worry," Bancroft told him. "She'll do it."

"And your stepdaughter?"

"My stepdaughter knows nothing about any of this."

"All right," Mason said. "I'll go to my office. You go on home and see what has happened. Keep me posted."

14

Della Street was waiting in the office when Mason arrived.

"Don't you ever go home?" Mason asked. "Do you have any idea what time it is?"

"I know," she said.

"Had anything to eat?"

"No."

"Well, let's see what we can do about that situation."

Della said, "You have someone waiting in the outer office."

"Who?" Mason asked.

"Someone I think you'll want to see, so I had him wait. Jetson Blair."

"The man who is going to marry Rosena Andrews?"

She nodded.

"What sort of a chap, Della?"

"A square-shooter; clean-cut, reserved—looks like a fine young fellow. Good breeding sticks out all over him and . . . well, he's just a prince."

"Apparently," Mason said, "he made quite an impression."

"He did," Della Street said, "and he's going to make the same impression on you."

"All right," Mason said, "let's talk with him. What does he want to see us about?"

"He said it was entirely personal and I didn't press him."

"Bring him in," Mason said, "and we'll press him, and then we'll go get something to eat."

Della vanished through the door to the outer office, returning with Jetson Blair, a tall individual with wavy, dark hair, cameolike features, steady eyes and the carriage of an athlete.

"This is Mr. Mason, Mr. Blair," she said.

Blair shook hands with the lawyer.

"What is it that you want?" Mason asked. "It is, of course, rather late and—"

"I know," Blair interrupted. "I've been waiting for quite a while. I'm sorry I have to present myself at this unconventional time and in such an unconventional manner, but after all my errand is unconventional."

Mason nodded. "Be seated," he said, "and let's see if we can get things straightened out."

Blair said, "I know enough from clues I have received here and there to put two and two together and make four."

"Go ahead," Mason said.

"That blackmail note was intended for Rosena," Blair said. "It was the first attempt on the part of blackmailers to squeeze some money out of a situation which could prove very embarrassing."

"What situation?" Mason asked.

"I believe that my brother, Carleton Blair, is still alive. I think that he has, perhaps, been involved in some things that would be very embarrassing to the family, to say the least."

"And so?" Mason said.

"And so, when I saw that article about the blackmail note and the money in the coffee can which had been picked up in the lake at a point which obviously was not too far from the Bancroft lake residence, I put two and two together."

"Go ahead," Mason said, tell me just what it is you want to get cleared up."

"Simply this," Blair said. "I am in love with Rosena, I think she is in love with me. If it turns out that there is a black sheep in the Blair family, we're going to have to face it. Blackmail doesn't ever solve anything. I don't want anybody to pay blackmail in order to spare the feelings of anyone in my family.

"If the scandal is such that Harlow Bancroft and Mrs. Bancroft don't feel that they can face it, then the wedding should be postponed or the engagement broken, if necessary."

"If they are willing to face it, I am willing to face it."

"How about your family?" Mason asked.

"I am satisfied my family will feel the same way. There is no use in giving in to blackmailers. That solves nothing."

"Have any demands been made on you in any way?" Mason asked.

"I really don't know," Jetson Blair said thoughtfully. "I received a telephone call from someone who asked me what I would say if I was told my brother was alive. The phone call was rather mysterious and I was naturally somewhat noncommittal."

"No attempt was made to fix a price or to suggest that information would be suppressed?" Mason asked.

"No. Nothing like that. It was a peculiar telephone conversation and the other party hung up abruptly."

"But it gave you something to think about?"

"Yes."

"Have you," Mason asked, "talked with Rosena about any of this?"

"No. I want to see her, but I wanted to see you first. I wanted to tell you that no matter what the situation is, I want to face it."

"Why did you come to me?" Mason asked.

"Because I understand from something Rosena told me that you were doing work for the family."

"And how does it happen you haven't talked with Rosena in detail about this?"

"I tried to see her last night but couldn't find her."

"You couldn't?"

"No."

"Where did you try to locate her?"

"At her apartment in town and at the house on the lake."

"And she wasn't there?"

"No."

"Had she told you she was going out?"

"No."

"And you don't know where she was?"

Blair said, "I phoned her today, Mr. Mason, and she told me that she felt something had happened that was going to have rather serious consequences and that she didn't want to talk to me for a while."

"By the way," Mason asked, "where were *you* last night when you tried to get in touch with her?"

"I tried first by telephone," Blair said, "and then I drove out to the lake house and then I drove to the apartment."

"Did you," Mason asked, "go to the yacht club?"

Blair hesitated, then met his eyes. "I did," he said.

"And find anything?"

Blair hesitated.

"Go ahead," Mason said.

"I found Mrs. Bancroft's car parked at the yacht club. I couldn't find Mrs. Bancroft and I couldn't find their yacht. I assumed therefore that she was out somewhere on the yacht. I thought perhaps Rosena might be with her mother. I asked some questions and was advised that Mrs. Bancroft had been there at the yacht club with a young man. I drove around the bay a bit and when I came back Mrs. Bancroft's car was gone. By that time a thick fog had settled down and it was impossible to see anything."

"Anyone with you?" Mason asked.

"No. I was alone."

"What time did you return home?"

"It was quite late."

"And you'd been trying to locate Rosena?"

"Yes."

Mason sighed, somewhat wearily. "All right," he said. "The police will probably be interrogating you. Don't try to conceal anything that you know, only don't tell the police anything that you have surmised. Just tell them the facts."

"The police?" Blair said. "What do they have to do with it? Will they be questioning me in connection with the blackmail?"

"They'll be questioning you in connection with your activities last night, what you know and where you went. They'll ask you what you have been told by any member of the Bancroft family."

"And what do I tell them?" Blair asked.

"The truth," Mason said, "but you don't tell them that you have taken two and two and made four. You give them the figures and let them make their own addition."

"The police are in on this blackmail business?" Blair asked.

Mason said, "The police are investigating another crime."

"Another crime! You mean there's something other than blackmail?"

Mason, his eyes on Blair's face, said, "I mean murder."

For a moment Blair was motionless. Then his face paled. "Murder?" he said.

"Murder," Mason said.

"But who? . . . What . . . ?"

"Someone took the Bancroft yacht last night and sailed it out into the harbor. Apparently the yacht drifted around for a while and came to rest at the upper end of the bay on some sand flats. When the sheriff boarded the boat this afternoon there was a body aboard it."

"A body!" Blair exclaimed. "Good heavens, not any one of the Bancrofts! Not—"

"No," Mason said, "the body of a young man. He may very well prove to be a young man with a criminal record."

"You mean—Carleton?"

"Not Carleton," Mason said. "Someone else."

"But how did the body get aboard the boat?"

"That," Mason said, "is anybody's guess. You've given me all the information you care to impart and I've given you all the information I *dare* to impart to you."

Mason arose and extended his hand. "Good night, Mr. Blair, and thank you for coming in."

Blair hesitated for a long moment, then gave Mason his hand.

The flesh was cold to the touch.

"Good night, Mr. Mason," he said, and moved out of the exit door, which Della Street held open for him, as though he were marching toward an execution chamber.

15

Newspaper headlines screamed across the top of the morning papers; BODY FOUND ON SOCIALITE'S YACHT—MAY TIE IN WITH BLACK-MAIL ATTEMPT—

The story dramatically played up the family, their silence which was attributed to an attempt to cover up the reason for extortion, and said all inquiries should be referred to Perry Mason, noted criminal attorney.

Della Street placed the morning newspapers on Mason's desk as he entered.

"Well," she said, "the press isn't *too* bad. So far, the police haven't intimated that any of the Bancrofts are directly suspected of murder, but their silence is supposed to connect up with the reason for the extortion note."

"That's good," Mason said.

"And," she said, "Mr. Bancroft has been in the outer office for the last fifteen minutes, waiting for you to come in."

"Bring him in," Mason said. "We'll see what's new at his end."

Bancroft evidently had passed a sleepless night. His face was gray with fatigue, the eyes lined with heavy pouches under the lower lids.

"How bad was it?" Mason asked.

"It was bad," Bancroft said, "but fortunately my wife was a real trouper. She said that she would only answer questions in the presence of her husband and in the presence of her attorney."

"And you?" Mason asked.

"I said the same."

"Did you give any reason for your silence?"

"Simply that there were certain things that we could not discuss at the present time; that at the proper time and in the proper place we would make a statement, but that we could not make a statement at the present time which would be aired in the public press."

Mason said, "All right, now we've got to go to work."

"Doing what?"

Mason said, "Your wife recognized the place where the boat ran aground?"

"Yes. It was right close to a wharf where we frequently get gas and oil. The wharf is closed during the night and apparently Gilly had planned to tie the boat up at this wharf but the dragging anchor caught before he quite got to the wharf."

"How deep was the water when your wife jumped overboard?"

"It was over her head—or she thinks it was, at first, but within a few swimming strokes she reached a point where she could put her feet on the bottom and walk ashore."

Mason said, "No gun was found on the boat. Your wife's purse wasn't found. Your wife feels that she dropped the purse and the gun as she jumped overboard."

"That's right. She thinks she heard the gun hit the deck and then bounce into the water. There was a splash."

"All right," Mason said, "what we have to do is locate that gun."

"*We* have!"

"That's right."

"Are you crazy?" Bancroft asked. "That is the one piece of evidence that we can't afford to have the police get their hands on. That gun is registered in my name, and if ballistics show it was the murder weapon—"

"Calm down," Mason said. "I didn't say we had to *recover* the gun, I said we had to *locate* it."

"You mean locate it and—"

"That's right," Mason said, "locate and leave it there in cold storage, so to speak."

"How are we going to do that?"

Mason said, "I want you to take a chart of the bay, pinpoint the location of the yacht. Paul Drake is going to have to take a diver out there and explore the bottom."

"And if he finds the gun and my wife's purse?"

"Drake," Mason said, "will say nothing until I tell him to."

"Isn't he supposed to report evidence to the police?"

"Drake won't know the significance of either the gun or the

purse," Mason said. "I'll see that he doesn't. He'll simply have a diver explore the floor of the bay at that point."

"But we *know* the stuff is there," Bancroft said. "There's no need to confirm it."

Mason regarded him with steady eyes. "You know your wife *told* you it was there," he said. "I'd like to confirm her statement."

"You don't doubt her word?"

Mason said, "When I'm handling a murder case I doubt everything and everybody—even you."

"But," Bancroft protested, "why do you have to *know* it's there?"

"Because," Mason said, "if your wife ever tells her story on the witness stand, we're going to demand that the sheriff send down a diver at that place and find the evidence which will corroborate her story."

"Well, you can do that without first checking the evidence."

"No, I can't," Mason said. "If I make that demand and a diver goes down there and the evidence *isn't* there, I've given your wife a one-way ticket to the gas chamber."

"But I tell you the evidence is there. It has to be. She jumped overboard, she had the strap of the purse over her wrist. She knows exactly where she jumped and—"

Mason said, "She's *never* going to tell her story unless she's *forced* to tell it on the witness stand. If she is forced to tell it, I want to be sure I can corroborate it."

"But when they find that gun— Don't you understand, Mason, the gun is registered in my name, and their ballistics department can prove it fired the fatal bullet. It ties the crime directly to Phyllis."

"Or to you," Mason said.

Bancroft was thoughtfully silent for a moment, then said, "How long before Drake will make his investigation?"

"It'll be done under cover of darkness," Mason said. "I want a diagram which pinpoints the location of that boat at the time your wife jumped overboard."

Bancroft seemed suddenly relieved. "You won't want it before tonight."

"I'll want the map early. Drake won't make the search until tonight."

"Okay," Bancroft said, "you'll have the map."

⊶ 16 ⊷

Shortly before noon Drake's code knock sounded on the dooı of Mason's private office.

Della Street let him in.

"Well," Drake said, "they've got the case pretty well buttoned up. The only trouble is they aren't sure just what they have in the net."

"Give," Mason said.

"Well, of course, Willmer Gilly's fingerprints gave him away. He's a grifter, a cheap chiseler, a car thief, an ex-con. He doesn't have a history of blackmail but he could very easily have gone in for blackmail.

"So they searched Gilly's apartment, which was really just a one room housekeeping affair with a little electric plate, a sink, a cupboard and a few dishes. Guess what they found."

"A Monarch Ten portable typewriter," Masun said.

"That's it," Drake said. "And they made a test run on the typewriter and found that the alignment of the letters and everything proved that the typewriter was the one that had been used by the person who wrote that blackmail note. So now they've tied the Bancrofts in with the blackmail note and Gilly in with the Bancrofts."

"Now then, they found something else."

"What?"

"That Mrs. Bancroft was down at the yacht club with Gilly during the early part of the evening."

"Hey, wait a minute!" Mason said. "Not Gilly, it was somebody else."

Drake shook his head. "The attendant has identified a photograph of Gilly and they are going to take him to the morgue to identify Gilly."

Mason frowned.

"That hits you hard?" Drake asked.

"That hits me hard," Mason said, "because it's one of those damned things that happen when the police force an identification. Mrs. Bancroft may have been down at the wharf with a young man but it wasn't Gilly. . . . I tell you what you do, Paul. There was a man named Irwin Fordyce who served time in San Quentin. Get mug shots of him from the police records. Get in touch with that attendant at the yacht club, show him the pictures of Fordyce and ask him if, as a matter of fact, Fordyce wasn't the man who was with Mrs. Bancroft."

"He's already made a positive identification," Drake said.

Mason frowned. "What about the time of death, Paul?"

"They fixed the time of death as nine o'clock."

"Wait a minute, wait a minute," Mason said, "they can't fix it at a definite hour when they didn't discover the body for some eighteen hours."

"Yes they can," Drake said. "They have traced Gilly's motions on the night of the murder. He had a meal consisting of canned beans which he had cooked himself in his little kitchen. The guy was a sloppy housekeeper and he was in a hurry so he didn't clean up after himself. He left part of the beans in the can, put them in the ice box, left the pan that the beans had been cooked in unwashed, and took off in a hurry—evidently in response to some telephone call. The coroner's been able to check the processes of digestion and pinpoint the time of death with relation to the last meal, with, of course, the usual hocus-pocus about body temperature, rigor mortis and postmortem lividity."

"No sign of the murder weapon?"

"No sign of the murder weapon, but they sure are trying to pin it on the Bancrofts. The records show that Bancroft had a permit for a .38-caliber revolver, and that seems to have disappeared."

Mason said, "Unless they can find that revolver and match it with ballistics they can't tie this crime to the Bancrofts. Not unless they can show an association with Gilly on the night of the murder. Now, that man at the yacht club is mistaken. Get busy immediately, Paul, and line up the mug shots of Irwin Fordyce. Then start work on that attendant at the yacht club. I've simply got to break down that identification; otherwise, we're in a hell of a shape."

"Then you're in a hell of a shape," Drake said, "because I don't think you're going to break it down."

"All right," Mason said, "now here's something else. I want a diver. I want a man of unquestioned integrity, someone who is perhaps the president of an amateur association of skin divers. I want a diving enthusiast, and I want him to do a job."

"When?"

"Just as soon as it gets dark," Mason said.

Drake frowned thoughtfully. "I have an operative who's a skin-diving enthusiast. He and his wife go out Sundays to—"

"Get them," Mason said.

"When?"

"Right away."

Drake looked at him thoughtfully. "You aren't going to use them to plant any evidence, Mason."

Mason said, "Get them. I'm not going to have them do anything unethical, if that's what's bothering you."

"All right," Drake said, "I'll get them. How soon?"

"Within an hour, if possible."

"Okay," Drake said, "we'll do the best we can."

Mason waited until Drake had left the office, then said to Della Street, "Go down to the bank, Della, and cash another three-thousand-dollar check. I want the money in fifties and hundred-dollar bills and I want the bank to retain the numbers of each bill."

"They're certainly going to wonder what's going on, after that other check for three thousand we cashed and asked for the number of the bills."

"I know," Mason said, "but when you're fighting for existence you have to use the weapons that come to hand. Try and keep them from getting any more suspicious than you have to, and above all I don't want any talk about it. Not to the police or anyone else. Just get the bills."

"Now?"

"Now."

"On my way," she said.

Within thirty minutes Della was back with the three thousand dollars in bills.

Within an hour Della Street said, "Mr. and Mrs. Chambers are in the office. They're the skin divers who work for Paul."

"Tell them to come in," Mason said.

Della Street brought the young couple into the office.

"Hello, Mr. Mason," the man said. "I'm Dunston Chambers. This is Lorraine, my wife. I understand you want some skin diving."

Mason sized them up, young people radiant with vitality and health.

"Your hobby seems to agree with you," Mason said.

Chambers grinned. "It does."

"I have a diving job I want done, and I want to be sure that no inkling of it leaks out anywhere."

"When?"

"Just as soon as it's possible to get under water without being detected."

"Where?"

"Down at Newport Harbor."

"I understand there's been a murder down there," Chambers said.

"Your understanding is correct," Mason told him.

"Does this have anything to do with the murder?"

"It has to do with the murder case."

"Are we clean?"

"You're clean."

"Okay, we're ready," Chambers said.

"We'll need a place to change," his wife pointed out.

"You do skin diving on week ends?"

"Yes."

"How do you change then?"

"We have a friend who has a cabin cruiser and—"

"Would he rent it?"

"Why . . . why, I suppose so."

"If you used that boat, could you do your diving where no one would know what was being done?"

"They'd know we were diving, but they wouldn't know where we were exploring. If the fog continues to hang on the water the way it's doing now, no one would know we were diving."

Mason nodded to the phone. "Get busy," he said. "See what you can fix up. Where are your outfits?"

"In the trunk of our car."

"And your car?"

"Downstairs."

Mason grinned and said, "Come on, we're going to hurry before that fog lifts."

—◄ 17 ►—

The thick blanket of fog clung to the calm surface of the water.

Chambers, at the wheel of the little cabin cruiser, said, "This is plenty thick, Mr. Mason."

"So much the better," Mason said.

"Now, just where do you want us?"

"That wharf over there," Mason said. "That oil and gas wharf. I want to arrange to tie up there and I want you to go overboard while we're tied up. I want you to comb every inch of the bottom, starting at a point about fifty feet to the south of the wharf, stretching from a point even with the end of the wharf down to water so shallow that a person can stand up in it.

"Now then, if you find *anything* unusual on the bottom I want you to leave it right where it is, but come and report to me."

"Okay," Chambers said, "if you'll take her in to the wharf, I'll go down and join Lorraine getting my things on."

Mason took the wheel and Chambers ducked down into the cabin.

Mason eased the boat alongside the wharf.

"Want gas?" the attendant asked.

Mason said, "I want to stay here for a little while."

"We only have facilities for berthing boats while they're putting on gas and oil."

"I know," Mason said, "you can put a gas hose out and fill the tanks. I'll pay for whatever gas you put in and give you twenty dollars extra just to leave the hose in the tank and pretend that we're still filling with gas."

"Say, what's the idea?" the attendant asked.

"Just making a survey," Mason said, "but it has to be handled in strict confidence."

"Okay," the attendant said. "I don't think many boats are going to be moving around in this fog. Gosh, it's thick. It's been bad for two-three days now."

"All right," Mason said. "Remember, no talking."

"No talking," the attendant said, with a grin.

A moment later Dunston and Lorraine Chambers appeared on deck, their tanks strapped to their backs. They adjusted their face masks, slipped over the side into the water.

Within ten minutes Dunston was back.

He climbed the ladder on the side of the yacht, took off the mask and said to Mason, "There's a woman's purse down there."

"Anything else unusual?" Mason asked.

"A woman's purse is all we found."

"Did you open the purse?"

"We're afraid something may float out of it if we open it."

"Bring the purse here," Mason said. "Leave your wife down there to mark the exact place. I want to look at the purse and then put it back."

Chambers hesitated a minute, then said, "Okay, orders are orders."

He again submerged and in a short time was back with the purse.

Mason squatted by the side of the rail. "Now, let's look at this purse," he said, "and inventory the contents."

The lawyer opened the purse.

"Good Lord, a roll of bills," Chambers said.

"Exactly," Mason said.

"And what the hell! A driving license. This is—"

Mason hastily interposed his hand between the card case and the diver's eyes. "Never mind," he said. "You're not supposed to see anything except what I show you. Now notice, I'm taking out this roll of bills and I'm substituting another roll of bills."

Mason took out the bills from the purse, took a roll of fifties and hundreds from his pocket, pushed it down into the purse and snapped the purse shut.

"Now then," he said, "take the purse back, put it right where it was and then start looking around for anything else that's unusual. Cover the floor of the bay for a space of a good hundred feet in every direction. What's the nature of the ground there, muddy or sandy?"

"Sandy. Oh, there's a little bit of ooze on top of it but for the most part it's a sandy silt."

"Okay," Mason said. "When you have covered the ground thoroughly, come back."

"And leave this purse down there?"

"Yes."

"With all that money?"

"With all that money. Only be sure to squeeze the air out of the purse so that it stays in that one place and doesn't float around any."

"There's enough junk in there, probably lipstick, keys and compact, to hold it down pretty well," Chambers said. "It's heavy."

"That's fine. Just squeeze the air out of it."

"And then what?"

"After you've ascertained that there's nothing else unusual on the floor of the bay there, come back."

Fifteen minutes later they were back at the boat.

"Everything okay?" Mason asked.

"Everthing okay."

"Nothing else unusual?"

"That's right. Nothing else unusual."

"That's fine," Mason said. "Go on down in the cabin and change your clothes."

Mason went over to the wharf, handed the attendant money for the gasoline, gave him an extra twenty dollars and said, "Thanks a lot. You can keep quiet?"

"Boy, can I keep quiet," the attendant said. "I can keep quiet in sixteen different languages including Scandinavian."

"English will be all you need for the time being," Mason told him, grinning.

18

At four-thirty Bancroft was back in Mason's office.

"Here," he said, "is a chart showing the exact position of the boat when my wife jumped overboard. You see this wharf, here. That's the oil and gas wharf. She estimates they were within thirty or forty feet of it when the anchor grabbed. The boat slued a little bit to the side and then started to drift. The tide was coming in at the time. She went overboard—"

"Which side?" Mason asked.

"The port side."

"That was the one away from the wharf?"

"Yes."

"All right," Mason said, "now get this straight. I don't want her to answer *any* questions. No questions by anybody. She is simply to state that her attorney will do the talking."

"Now, wait a minute," Bancroft said. "I wanted to talk to you about that. As some of the newspapers have pointed out, that's the poorest way to win public support. It makes everyone think she's guilty right at the start."

"I know," Mason said. "Newspaper reporters get paid for the stories they get and publish. They want a story. They're using all the arguments in the world."

"But those arguments are logical, Mason."

"Of course they're logical," Mason said. "They're right. You can't argue with logic."

"Then why can't she tell her story now?"

"Because," Mason said, "she's fighting a combination of circumstances that may prove too much for her if we're not careful. Do you realize that the yachting attendant is going to testify that she went down on the wharf with Willmer Gilly earlier in the evening and personally took him out aboard the boat?"

"What!" Bancroft explained.

"That's a fact," Mason said.

"Why, he's crazy. That was Irwin Fordyce who was with her."

"And where's Irwin Fordyce now?"

"I don't know. No one knows."

"All right," Mason said. "That yachting attendant has made an identification of Gilly as the—"

"Why, he *couldn't* have," Bancroft interrupted. "Why, that near-sighted old fuddy-duddy—you mean Drew Kirby?"

"I don't know his name," Mason said. "He's the yachting attendant there."

"That's Drew Kirby. Why, that old— Why, that's crazy."

"It may be crazy," Mason said, "but he's made the identification. Now, you and your wife are going to have to do just as I tell you. I don't want your wife to tell her story to anyone until I tell her to relate the story. Then it's going to be told under the most dramatic circumstances possible and *then* we're going to send divers down and find the purse and the gun."

"Suppose the— Well, suppose the action of the tides or something has caused the purse and the gun to drift away?"

"I don't think that'll happen," Mason said. "This is in a pretty sequestered part of the bay. The tide action is relatively gentle. We haven't had any winds and—"

"You're taking an awful chance," Bancroft said.

"*We're* taking an awful chance," Mason agreed gravely, "but we're going to have to play the cards the way they're dealt to us and we've got to play them to the best advantage."

Bancroft said, "All right, Mason, I'll rely on your judgment. There's nothing else I can do."

"That's right," Mason told him. "There's nothing else you can do."

19

Judge Cole S. Hobart called the court to order.

"The case of the People versus Phyllis Bancroft," he said. "The People are represented by Robley Hastings, district attorney, and Turner Garfield, deputy district attorney; the defendant is represented by Mr. Perry Mason. Gentlemen, are you ready to proceed with the preliminary hearing?"

"The People are ready," Hastings said.

"The defendant is ready," Mason said.

"Very well, proceed," Judge Hobart said. "Now, I notice that this trial has attracted a lot of attention in the public press. I warn the spectators that I want quiet in the courtroom. There will be no demonstrations. People will be permitted to leave the courtroom during the progress of the trial provided they do so in an orderly manner.

"Proceed with your case, Mr. District Attorney."

Turner Garfield took over the preliminaries. He called a surveyor and introduced a map of the harbor, aerial photographs of the bay and the yacht club, and a road map of the county showing distances between various points.

"Cross-examine," Garfield said to Mason.

Mason said to the surveyor, "You have introduced these various maps but I noticed there is one map which you have failed to introduce."

"What is that?"

"A coast geodetic chart of the harbor."

"I didn't consider that was necessary because the various maps which I have introduced are accurate and the aerial photograph gives a picture of the coast line and the boundaries of the harbor. The chart, on the other hand, is marked with various figures showing the depth of the water in feet and fathoms and I felt these might be confusing."

"Why?"

"There are figures on charts which have nothing to do with the case or the indentation of the shore line and I thought they might be confusing."

"But you do have a geodetic survey chart with you?"

"Not with me, no."

"Then I show you one," Mason said, "and ask you if you are familiar with it."

"Yes, certainly."

"That is an official chart, made by the government?"

"Yes."

"And is used in navigation and is accurate?"

"I believe it is very accurate."

"I would like to have that introduced as defendant's exhibit Number One," Mason said.

"We have no objection on earth," Turner Garfield said. "Anything in the line of statistical information that the defense wants introduced in this case may be introduced."

The next witness was the sheriff of Los Angeles County.

Garfield said, "Sheriff, I show you a photograph, one of the People's exhibits, showing a body which has been identified as the body of a man found shot to death on the yacht, *Jinesa*, and ask you if you recognize the photograph."

"I do."

"Have you seen the person shown in that photograph?"

"Several times."

"Dead or alive?"

"Both."

"You have seen him alive?"

"Several times."

"And you saw him dead?"

"Yes, I went to the morgue here and looked at the body."

"Did you make any further attempt to identify the body?"

"I did."

"What?"

"I took fingerprints."

"Are you prepared to identify that body?"

"I am."

"Whose body is it?"

"That of Willmer Gilly."

"Cross-examine," Garfield said.

"What were your standards of comparison as far as fingerprints are concerned, Sheriff?" Mason asked.

"FBI records."

"Gilly, then, had a criminal record?"

"Objected to as being incompetent, irrelevant and immaterial," Robley Hastings, the district attorney said.

"Overruled," Judge Hobart said. "The sheriff was asked about fingerprints and I think counsel is entitled to interrogate him on the authenticity of the fingerprints and how he happened to have them and all matters in connection with them. The Court is going to give the defendant the greatest latitude in the field of cross-examination. Answer the question, Sheriff."

"He had a criminal record, yes."

"For what?"

"Stealing an automobile and forgery."

"Any other record?"

"No other convictions, no."

"Had he, to your knowledge, been arrested in cases where there were no convictions?"

"Again I have to interpose an objection," the district attorney said.

"Overruled," Judge Hobart snapped. "The sheriff stated he saw the decedent several times when he was alive and counsel certainly has a right to interrogate as to any such occasion."

"But, if the Court please," Hobart persisted, "a witness can only be impeached by showing that he has been convicted of a felony, not that he has been arrested and charged with crime and then either acquitted or the proceedings dismissed."

"Counsel is not trying to impeach a dead man," Judge Hobart said. "He is trying to test the recollection of a witness. However, since counsel can quite readily reframe the question I will sustain the objection."

"To save any question," Mason said, "I'll reframe the question to show exactly what I am getting at.

"Sheriff, on some of the occasions when you saw the decedent, Willmer Gilly, he was under arrest?"

"Yes."

"And you saw him in your official capacity?"

"Yes."

"Did you make any of those arrests?"

"One."

"On what charge?"

"Objected to as incompetent, irrelevant and immaterial and not proper cross-examination," Hastings said.

"The objection is sustained," Judge Hobart ruled.

"No further questions," Mason said.

Robley Hastings, with something of a dramatic gesture, said, "I call Drew Kirby to the stand."

Kirby proved to be a slow-moving, grizzled individual in his fifties with watery blue eyes, an habitual squint and a leather-skinned face —the skin weatherbeaten to a deep, permanent tan.

"Where are you employed?" Hastings asked.

"At the Blue Sky Yacht Club."

"Where is that?"

"That's down on the bay."

"Now, by the bay you mean what bay?"

"Well, Newport-Balboa Bay."

"And how long have you been employed there?"

"For four years."

"Consistently?"

"That's right."

"What are your duties?"

"I'm a general roustabout and caretaker. I sort of keep things running, keep track of things for the members, occasionally row them back and forth to yachts—them and their friends."

"Were you so employed on the tenth of this month?"

"I was."

"On the evening of the tenth?"

"Yes, sir."

"I'm going to show you a picture of Willmer Gilly, one of the People's exhibits, and ask you if you have ever seen him before."

"Yes, sir."

"Alive or dead?"

"Both."

"To the best of your recollection, when did you see him first?"

"It was around seven o'clock, I guess, on the tenth."

"Where was he?"

"Down at the yacht club."

"Who was he with, or who was with him?"

"Mrs. Bancroft was with him."

"Now, by Mrs. Bancroft you mean Phyllis Bancroft, the defendant in this action, the woman sitting to the left of Perry Mason?"

"Yes, sir."

"And where was she?"

"She was out on the landing—the float."

"And what was she doing?"

"Well, she was getting in a dinghy that belonged to the Bancroft yacht, the *Jinesa.*"

"Did you see her talking to Gilly?"

"Oh, yes, she was talking to him."

"And what happened?"

"She rowed him out to the yacht."

"She rowed him, or he did the rowing?"

"Well, she rowed him out and put him aboard the yacht."

"Then what?"

"They were aboard the yacht for about ten or fifteen minutes, I guess, I don't know. I didn't see them after they got aboard the yacht. Then I saw her rowing back."

"Alone?"

"Yes, sir. Alone."

"Then what?"

"Well, she left the dinghy tied up at the float and went off somewhere and I saw her come back after a while, I guess it was maybe an hour."

"And what was she doing then?"

"Well, she had some packages in a shopping bag."

"And what did she do?"

"Got in the dinghy and rowed out to the yacht."

"And then what happened?"

"Well, now there I don't know what happened, sir. I was busy for a while and a thick fog had come in, one of those real heavy, pea-soup fogs. You couldn't see a darn thing—that is, I mean you couldn't see out in the bay, at all."

"Could you see as far as the yacht, the *Jinesa?*"

"No, sir."

"And what did you do?"

"Well, I was busy around the place."

"When did the fog lift?"

"It didn't lift. It just settled down heavy."

"Well, it must have lifted some time," Hastings said, his manner showing annoyance.

"Oh, sure, it cleared up the next afternoon."

"And when did you next see the Bancroft yacht, the *Jinesa*?"

"I didn't see it. It was gone."

"But you did see it again?"

"Oh, sure. About—I don't know, I guess it was about four-thirty or so the next afternoon they came bringing it in."

"What do you mean, they?"

"The sheriff and some deputies."

"How did they bring it in?"

"They were towing it with another boat."

"What other boat?"

"A Coast Guard boat."

"And what was done then?"

"Well, they cleared off a place at the float and tied the boat up and roped off the float, and then a lot of photographers and police officers came aboard."

"Now, did you see Willmer Gilly after his death?"

"Yes, sir."

"Where?"

"At the county morgue."

"You were taken there to look at the body?"

"Yes, sir."

"And was that the same body, that is, the body of the same man that you had seen on the evening of the tenth with the defendant, Mrs. Bancroft?"

"Yes, sir."

"You're positive?"

"Yes, sir."

"Is there any slightest shadow of doubt in your mind?"

"No, sir."

"You may cross-examine," Hastings said to Perry Mason.

Mason arose from his chair at the counsel table, walked over to stand in front of the witness, whom he regarded with a kindly air and said conversationally, "You've identified this photograph of Willmer Gilly."

"That's right."

"When did you first see a photograph of Gilly?"

"I saw Gilly himself."

"I know," Mason said, "but when was the first time you saw a *photograph* of Gilly?"

"Well, that was when they came looking around— Let me see, that was— Why, yes, that was about nine o'clock, I guess, on the night of the eleventh."

"How long after the yacht had been brought in to the float?"

"Oh, I don't know, four or five hours, I guess."

"Who showed you the picture?"

"The sheriff."

"Ask you if you'd ever seen him before?"

"Something like that."

"Actually, didn't the sheriff ask you if that wasn't a photograph of a man that had been with Mrs. Bancroft the night before, and ask you if you hadn't seen her row him out to the boat?"

"Something like that, I guess."

"Do you remember the sheriff's exact words?"

"Well, no. He showed me the photograph. He said he thought I probably had seen the man."

"Did you agree with him?"

"I told him I might have, yes."

"Did he ask you to study the photograph carefully?"

"Yes."

"Did you?"

"Yes."

"That was before you went to the morgue to look at the body?"

"Yes."

"When did you go to the morgue?"

"On the evening of the twelfth."

"How many times had you seen Gilly's picture before you went to the morgue?"

"Oh, several times."

"How many?"

"Quite a few."

"Did you have a copy of the picture in your possession?"

"I had a print, yes."

"Where did you get it?"

"The sheriff gave it to me."

"Told you to study it carefully?"

"Yes."

"Told you he wanted you to identify the man in the photograph?"

"Oh, I don't think he said it that way. He asked me if that wasn't the man that had been down there on the float with Mrs. Bancroft the night before and I told him it sure looked like it."

"And he left you the photograph and told you to study it?"

"Not right away. That was the next morning."

"The morning of the twelfth?"

"Yes."

"And you studied that picture off and on during the day?"

"Yes."

"And then after you'd studied the picture you were taken to the morgue."

"That's right."

Mason regarded the man thoughtfully. "Did you have your glasses on when you looked at the picture?"

"Sure."

"Where are your glasses now?"

The witness reached automatically for his breast pocket, then took his hand away and said, "I left them down in my room."

"But on the eleventh and twelfth when you looked at the picture you had your glasses on, is that right?"

"Yes."

"You can see better with your glasses on?"

"Naturally."

"Could you have identified the picture without your glasses?"

"I don't know. I don't think so."

"But you identified the picture here in the courtroom without glasses."

"I knew whose picture it was."

"How did you know whose picture it was?"

"Well, it had to be the picture of this dead man."

"What do you mean, it had to be?"

"Well, it was, wasn't it?"

"I'm asking you," Mason said. "Do you know whose picture it was?"

"Yes. I swore to it, didn't I?"

"And you can see it without your glasses?"

"Yes."

Mason walked over to the exhibit, picked it up, took another photograph from his pocket, compared them for a moment, then approached the witness and said, "Now look at this photograph. Are you positive that's the man that was with the defendant on the night of the tenth?"

"I told you I'm positive."

"That's the man?"

"Yes."

"No question of doubt in your mind?"

"No."

"Just a moment, just a moment," Hastings shouted, jumping to his feet. "Counsel has two photographs there, one that he's taken from his pocket while we couldn't see what he was doing."

"All right," Mason said, "I'll show the witness both photographs. These are both photographs of the same person?"

"Yes."

"Let me see that photograph," Hastings said.

"Certainly," Mason said, handing the district attorney the two photographs.

"Now, wait a minute, wait a minute," Hastings said. "This isn't being fair to the witness. These are two different photographs."

"He's just sworn they're photographs of the same person," Mason said.

"Well, I submit that the witness should be advised . . ."

"Advised of what?" Mason said.

"That this second photograph is not a photograph of Willmer Gilly."

Mason turned to the witness. "Do you see any difference in these pictures, Mr. Kirby?"

The witness squinted his eyes, took the photographs, held his head back a ways and said, "They look the same to me but I don't see so good without any glasses."

"Do you wear your glasses all the time?"

"Sure."

"Why didn't you wear them today?"

"Well . . ."

"Why?" Mason asked.

"Well, I left them down at my room at the club."

"Did anyone suggest that you might leave your glasses there?"

"Well, I was told that if I came in here wearing glasses and tried to make an identification that they'd make things pretty rough for me."

"Why?"

"Well, they just said that it would be pretty rough for me."

"Who said that?"

"The district attorney."

"And told you to leave your glasses down at the yacht club?"

"He said it might be a good plan."

"That," Mason said, "was because you weren't wearing the glasses on the night of the tenth, isn't that right?"

"Well, you can't wear glasses around water when a fog is coming in. It's better not to have anything on at all. You can see clearer without glasses than you can with glasses. You take a lot of fog coming in and it gets all over the lenses and you just keep wiping it off and wiping it off and it's better not to have them."

"So you weren't wearing glasses on the night of the tenth?"

"I told you it was foggy. The fog was coming in."

"Then when you saw the man whom you later identified as Willmer Gilly, you weren't wearing your glasses?"

"I told you I didn't have them on while I was out there on the float. How many times do I have to tell you that?"

"But I'm just trying to check with your testimony," Mason said patiently. "You didn't have them on when you first saw Gilly."

"No."

"Not at any time?"

"No."

"Not when you saw the defendant?"

"No—but I recognized her all right."

"Certainly you recognized her all right," Mason said, "because you've known her for years. But you didn't have your glasses on when you looked at these two pictures and you certainly testified that they were pictures of the same individual.

"Now, if the Court please, I wish to have the second picture marked for identification. That is a picture which I intend to connect up later on and I would like to have it marked for identification as defendant's exhibit Number Two."

"So ordered," Judge Hobart said.

"I object to this type of cross-examination," Hastings said. "This is the old razzle-dazzle for which counsel is noted. It's a method of getting a witness mixed up."

Mason smiled at the judge. "I'm not the one who asked him to leave his glasses down at the yacht club, Your Honor. The witness identified a picture which had been introduced in evidence by the People as that of Willmer Gilly, the person who was down at the yacht club on the night of the tenth with the defendant. I simply handed him two pictures and asked him if they were both pictures of the same person and he said they were."

"The record speaks for itself," Judge Hobart said. "The second picture may be marked for identification as defendant's exhibit Number Two."

"I can see all right without my glasses," Kirby said. "I don't wear them lots of times when I'm down there around the water, particularly at night."

"I understand," Mason said. "When the moisture gets on the lenses they're something of a nuisance."

"That's right."

"And since it was a foggy night on the night of the tenth you had the glasses off."

"Well, it wasn't real foggy the first part of the night but it was moist and damp, and then of course when the fog came in it wouldn't have made any difference if you'd had a pair of binoculars on. You couldn't see anything. That is, at any distance."

"Thank you," Mason said. "I have no further questions."

Hastings hesitated for a long moment, then said, "No redirect."

"Call your next witness," Judge Hobard instructed.

"I'll call Sheriff Jewett, the sheriff of Orange County, to the stand," Hastings said.

Sheriff Jewett testified to having received a report from his deputy that a yacht was aground at the upper end of the bay, that a body was in it, that he went to the scene, arriving there about four o'clock in the afternoon. That he boarded the yacht, found the body, that a Coast Guard boat was standing by, and they took the yacht in tow and towed it to the Blue Sky Yacht Club where it was moored so that the boat could be searched for fingerprints and clues. That photographs were taken, that the body of Willmer Gilly was lying on its stomach facing the after portion of the boat, that the body was in the main navigating cabin, that there was a bullet hole in the heart. That he had subsequently supervised the removal of the body to the county morgue, that there an autopsy surgeon had recovered a bullet from the body, that the sheriff had taken charge of that bullet which he identified and which was introduced in evidence.

"You identified the body?" Hastings asked.

"Yes, sir. The body was that of Willmer Gilly."

"Did you find where the decedent had been living prior to his death."

"Yes, sir."

"Where was it?"

"It was in the Ajax-Delsey Apartments. That is called an apartment house, actually it is more of a rooming house with limited cooking facilities in most of the rooms."

"Did you visit the decedent's room or apartment in that house?"

"I did."

"What did you find?"

"I found an iron bedstead with a rather thin, lumpy mattress, four army blankets, two pillows, two straightback chairs, one overstuffed chair, a toilet, a sink, a small shower, a few dishes, a two-burner electric plate."

"Were there sheets on the bed?"

"There were no sheets."

"A case on the pillow?"

"No pillowcase. A turkish towel had been placed over the pillow and it was quite soiled."

"Was there a clothes closet?"

"No, sir. There was a small alcove across which a three-foot length of pipe had been stretched and half a dozen wire coat hangers had been placed on that pipe. Three of the coat hangers had clothes on them, some slacks, a pair of overalls and a sports coat."

"Anything else?"

"Yes, sir. In a hamper I found a skin-diving outfit complete with tanks. Acting on information contained in a label on the suit and the tanks, I found that the outfit had been rented from the Valley View Skin Diving Outfitters. Rent had been paid for a week."

"What else did you find?"

"I found a somewhat rickety kitchen table on which was a bottle of catsup, a plate, which had contained canned beans, knife, fork and spoon and a coffee cup. There was a small electric ice box in which there was a quart carton of milk half full, a can of pork and beans about half empty, about half of a quarter pound of butter and about half a pound of raw hamburger.

"Above this ice box was a small cupboard which contained two cans of pork and beans, one can of chili con carne, a small bottle of Tobasco sauce, a pound container of sugar about half empty, two water tumblers, two coffee cups and saucers, four plates, two tin pie plates, a cream pitcher with a broken handle.

"In a drawer in a table there were some knives, forks and spoons, three of each. There was one frying pan, one rather battered aluminum sauce pan which had apparently been used to warm up the beans. It was still on the stove, and though the beans had been scraped out of it there were traces of canned beans still adhering to the pot. There was half a loaf of sliced bread on the table."

"Was there any tablecloth?"

"No."

"Anything else?"

"I've mentioned everything I can remember at the moment in the line of orthodox furnishings," the sheriff said, "but I took a complete set of photographs showing the apartment as we found it."

"Nothing had been disturbed when those photographs were taken?"

"No, sir. We took photographs showing everything in the apartment."

"Those photographs were taken by you or under your supervision?"

"Yes, sir."

"We ask that these twelve photographs be introduced in evidence and given appropriate numbers," Hastings said.

"No objection," Mason said.

"Now then," Hastings said, "returning to this bullet, the so-called fatal bullet, which you have identified. What caliber was that?"

"A .38 caliber."

"Could you tell from the direction of the groove marks what make of gun had discharged that?"

"Yes, it was fired from a gun which had the same rifling marks as a Smith and Wesson revolver."

"Sheriff, did you ask the defendant if she knew anything about a .38-caliber Smith and Wesson revolver?"

"I did."

"Did you receive any answer?"

"She said that she was under instructions to say nothing to anyone, that at the proper time she would tell her story and until then she had nothing to say."

"Did you ask her husband, Harlow Bancroft, about a gun?"

"Yes."

"What did he say?"

"He made virtually the same answer."

"Did you search the firearms registry to see if he had purchased a weapon?"

"I did."

"What did you find?"

"That on the fifteenth day of June of last year he had purchased a Smith and Wesson .38-caliber revolver, No. 133347."

"Did you ask him to produce that gun for you?"

"I did."

"What was his answer?"

"He said that the gun was not available."

"Did you ask him to explain that remark?"

"I did."

"Did he give you any explanation?"

"No, sir."

"Now then, directing your attention to furnishings other than what you have called orthodox in the apartment of the decedent, Willmer Gilly, did you find anything under the bed?"

"Yes, sir, I did."

"What was it?"

"A Monarch Ten portable typewriter."

"Did you have occasion to use this typewriter?"

"Yes, sir, I ran off the alphabet, both upper and lower case, on a sheet of paper."

"Now, Sheriff, I show you what purports to be a note demanding the payment of three thousand dollars, which is to be placed in a red coffee can in accordance with subsequent instructions which are to be telephoned, and ask you if you recognize that note."

"I do, yes, sir."

"When did you first see that note?"

"It was handed to me by a lifeguard employed at a public swimming beach at Lake Merticito. He said it had been given him by a young—"

"Never mind what he said," Hastings interrupted hastily, "that's hearsay. But I will ask you whether you compared the typewriting on that note with the sample of typewriting you had taken from the Monarch Ten portable typewriter you had found in the room of the decedent, Willmer Gilly?"

"I did, yes, sir."

"With what result?"

"Studying the alignment of the letters and a chipped type face, I became convinced there was no question but that this so-called blackmail note had been written on the typewriter which we found in Willmer Gilly's room."

"Returning now to the fatal bullet," Hastings said, "did you make any attempt to match that bullet with any other bullet?"

"I did, yes, sir."

"With what other bullets?"

"Harlow Bancroft owns a mountain cottage some thirty miles out of San Bernardino in the high mountains. I went to that lodge, or house, and looked around. The house is situated on property which comprises a little over two acres. In back of the house I found a target made of four thicknesses of Celotex, backed with a two-inch board. This target in turn had been placed upright against an embankment."

"What else did you find?"

"I pried the Celotex loose from the board and found quite a number of bullets imbedded in the board. Most of these bullets were of .22 caliber, but three of them were .38-caliber bullets. I carefully excavated around the target and sifted the soil and found a large number of bullets, mostly of .22 caliber, but again I found half a dozen .38-caliber bullets."

"Now then, do you have in your office a so-called comparison microscope?"

"Yes, sir, I do."

"This is a microscope used in matching bullets?"

"Yes, sir."

"Did you compare the fatal bullet, which has been introduced in evidence, with any of the bullets you recovered from the Bancroft property?"

"Yes, sir, I compared them all."

"With what result?"

"I found two bullets in good enough shape to make a comparison."

"With what result?"

"Both of those bullets had been fired from the same gun which had fired the fatal bullet."

"Did you make photographs showing the fatal bullet superimposed upon these recovered bullets?"

"I did, yes, sir. Here are the photographs showing how the striations match perfectly. The fatal bullet is the one above and the recovered bullets are those below."

"Each of these three photographs represents a different recovered bullet?"

"That is right. The top bullet in each photograph is the fatal bullet, or rather the top portion of the fatal bullet. The lower bullet is in each case the lower portion of one of the three recovered bullets."

"We ask that these three photographs be received in evidence," Hastings said.

"No objection," Mason said.

Hastings turned to Mason with a triumphant smile. "Would you care to cross-examine?" he asked.

"Oh," Mason said casually, "I have a few questions."

Mason advanced to stand in front of the sheriff.

"You have stated that the so-called blackmail note was written on this Monarch Ten portable which you found in the room of the decedent?"

"Yes, sir."

"The *entire* note was written on that typewriter?"

"I can't swear to every single letter of every single word, because I'm a law enforcement officer and not an expert on questioned documents, but I did find a couple of defective type faces on that typewriter and I found those same defects on those same letters in the note, so on the strength of that I know the note was written on that typewriter."

"What time was it when you got to the yacht, *Jinesa*? That is, you yourself, personally?" Mason asked.

"Three-fifty-five P.M.," the sheriff said.

"The Coast Guard cutter was standing by?"

"Yes, sir."

"You had previously been notified by telephone?"

"Yes, sir."

"And had proceeded immediately to the place where the yacht was found?"

"Yes, sir."

"Now, was the yacht aground at the time it was discovered?"

The sheriff stroked his chin. "Frankly, I don't know," he said. "I think it was. It was floating when I arrived. The tide, I believe, was going out then."

"Was the boat anchored?"

"There was an anchor out, yes."

"With how much chain?"

"Well, with not very much chain. Only a few feet."

"What do you mean by a few feet, eight feet? Ten feet? Twenty feet?"

"I would say somewhere around fifteen to twenty feet, yes."

"And you moved the yacht?"

"I ordered it moved so we could get our paraphernalia and equipment aboard. We had to."

"Did you mark the exact place where the yacht was when you found it?"

"Well, not the exact place, no. Of course, I know approximately."

"But with twenty feet of anchor chain out you couldn't tow the yacht."

"We picked up the anchor and dropped it aboard the yacht."

"And then towed it."

"Yes."

"And you don't know the exact place where the yacht was located?"

"I know approximately."

"But not exactly."

"Well, I couldn't put it right back in *exactly* the same place, no."

"What was the tide at that time?"

"I don't know for sure. It was going out, but I think it was high, pretty high."

"Did you ever return to that place at low tide to search the ground adjacent to the place where the yacht was found?"

"No."

"Why not?"

"Because nobody had been aboard that boat for some time. It had floated with the tide. It floated in there and to a point where the anchor engaged the bottom of the bay."

"How do you know?"

"Because of various and sundry discoveries we made. The dinghy was still fastened to the yacht and the anchor had been just dragging along at the end of about fifteen or twenty feet of chain."

"How do you know that?"

"By circumstantial evidence."

"How do you know the yacht hadn't been taken to that point and anchored there?"

"There was no reason to anchor it there."

"But someone might have had some reason to anchor it there?"

"We made a careful search of the shore line. We found no indications that any boat had landed. We decided the yacht had drifted with a dragging anchor line to the place where it finally came to rest at high tide."

"That was just your conclusion?"

"From circumstantial evidence, yes."

"You don't know now *exactly* where you found the boat?"

"Certainly I do. We found it out about three hundred and fifty yards from—"

"Did you measure it?" Mason interrupted.

"No."

"When you say about three hundred and fifty yards you're making just an estimate?"

"Yes."

"You couldn't go back and pinpoint the exact location of that place?"

"No, I have already said that."

"Do you know how long the boat had been there when you found it?"

"It had drifted in on the high tide. I assume that it had *probably* drifted in on the tide the night before."

"What is the basis of that assumption, Sheriff?"

"We know almost exactly when Gilly met his death. He had been seen on the club landing. He had been taken aboard the yacht. He had eaten canned beans at his apartment. Death had been within approximately two hours of the time he had his last meal. The yacht had evidently been drifting aimlessly with the tide. There was virtually no wind."

Mason said, "Let's just check those tides, Sheriff. I show you a tide table. You will note it shows that high tide on the tenth actually took place on the early morning of the eleventh, at one-fifteen A.M."

"That is correct."

"The next high tide was at two-thirty-two on the afternoon of the eleventh."

"That's right, yes, sir."

"And you found the boat at low tide?"

"The tide was dropping very rapidly. It was not quite low tide."

"And you promptly hooked onto the boat and towed it in to the float?"

"After I got there I ordered it towed in to where we could go to work on it, yes."

"That's all," Mason said.

Hastings said, "If the Court please, I am now going to call another witness, Stilson L. Kelsey. This man is partially hostile. I canuot vouch for him but I want his testimony because it is vital."

"Very well," Judge Hobart said. "Mr. Kelsey to the stand."

Kelsey presented a somewhat different appearance from the man Mason had seen at Eve Amory's apartment. He had had a haircut, his suit was new, his shoes were new. He had an air of complete assurance.

"What is your name?" the district attorney asked.

"Stilson L. Kelsey."

"What if your occupation?"

"I refuse to answer."

"On what grounds?"

"On the grounds that the answer will incriminate me."

"Are you acquainted—or were you acquainted—with the decedent, Willmer Gilly, during his lifetime?"

"I was."

"Did you have any business arrangements with him?"

"I did."

"Did you have any arrangements with him concerning a business transaction which was to culminate on the evening of the tenth?"

"Yes, sir, I did."

"On the tenth of this month what was your occupation, Mr. Kelsey? Now, that question is limited to the tenth of the month."

"Well, I didn't have any *regular* occupation."

"How were you making your living?"

Kelsey took a deep breath, said, "I received donations from various people."

"Come on, speak up," Hastings said. "What was the nature of the occupation? What caused those donations?"

Kelsey shifted his position, crossed his legs and said, "Blackmail."

"And did you have any arrangement with Willmer Gilly covering the blackmail of any member of the Bancroft family?"

"Objected to as incompetent, irrelevant and immaterial," Mason said.

"We propose to connect it up. We propose to show motive," Hastings said. "This witness is a key witness in the case. He has turned State's evidence as to this particular transaction. His testimony is going to be most important and most significant. I am willing to waive blackmail in order to clear up a murder."

"I'll overrule the objection," Judge Hobart said. "The Court would like to get to the bottom of this. Go ahead."

"Answer the question," Hastings said.

Kelsey said, "Gilly came to me with a story."

"What was the story?"

"Objected to as hearsay," Mason said.

"I propose to show it is part of the *res gestae*," Hastings said.

Judge Hobart frowned. "Does this story have to do with your business relations with Gilly?"

"Yes, Your Honor."

"I'm going to allow the testimony," Judge Hobart said. "It may be I will strike it out after I hear it, but I am going to allow it subject to a motion to strike."

Kelsey said, "Gilly had become very friendly with a man in the same rooming house where he was living."

"What was the rooming house?"

"The Ajax-Delsey Apartments."

"All right, go ahead."

"Well, Gilly said that he had become very friendly with a man named Irwin Victor Fordyce; that Fordyce had a past and that he finally confided his story to Gilly; that Gilly was the only one that he had ever told; that he told Gilly the story because of friendship with Gilly and because he felt he could trust Gilly's discretion."

"Now, did you take action on that story—as a result of that story?"

"I did."

"That action was directly responsible for the joint business association you had with Mr. Gilly?"

"It was."

"Generally, what was the story?"

"Objected to," Mason said, "as hearsay. Incompetent, irrelevant and immaterial."

"Overruled. I'm going to hear it," Judge Hastings said, "subject to a motion to strike."

"Well," Kelsey said, "it seems that Fordyce was an assumed name, that the man who went under the name of Fordyce was related to someone very high socially and if the true identity of Fordyce and his criminal record became known, the very high society wedding between Rosena Andrews, a member of the Bancroft family, and Jetson Blair, a member of the socially prominent Blair family, would never come off."

"So what was done?"

"Without anything being said that would let Fordyce have any idea we were acting on the information, Gilly and I decided to use the information for our own benefit and turn it into money."

"Now, what did you do with relation to that decision?"

"Well, I looked up the families a little bit and found the Bancroft family was lousy with money and the Blair family was stronger on social position than money. I felt that it would be easy to get some money out of the Bancroft family."

"How much money?"

"Fifteen hundred dollars in one bite, a thousand in another."

"That was all you intended to get?"

"Certainly not. We intended to test out the information that we had. We figured that fifteen hundred dollars and a second payment of a grand would be enough to make it worth while, but not too much to cause undue alarm on the part of Rosena Andrews. We felt that we'd just see how good the tip was. If she was willing to pay fifteen hundred dollars, and her mother another thousand, then we'd wait a week or so and put the bite on her for more and then keep crowding her until we found just what the limit was. At least that was the understanding Gilly and I had."

"All right, what happened?"

"Well, we wrote a blackmail note and put it on the front seat of Rosena Andrews' car. We didn't want to send it through the mail. Gilly had a typewriter and was a good typist. I couldn't run one of the things. So Gilly wrote the note. He showed me the note, however, and it met with my approval."

"And what were the terms of the note?"

"That Rosena had to pay fifteen hundred dollars in accordance with instructions that we would give over the telephone unless she wanted to have the information made public that would disgrace the family."

"That was intended in the nature of a trial balloon?" Hastings asked.

"That's right. And then Gilly contacted the defendant and put the same story up to her and she decorated the mahogany with a thousand. Neither knew the other had been milked on a shakedown."

"Go ahead. Then what happened?"

"Well, we kept watch until we were sure Rosena had got her note. She got in the automobile and saw the note on the front seat and picked it up, looked at it, read it a couple of times and then drove off."

"Then what happened?"

"Well," Kelsey said ruefully, "without my knowledge, after I had seen the note, Gilly apparently had crossed out the fifteen hundred dollars and put the bite on her for three thousand."

"Without telling you?"

"Without telling me."

"What was the object of that?" Hastings asked.

"He was trying to cut himself another fifteen hundred dollars. You see, according to the way we figured out our instructions, we'd take a boat out on the lake—the Bancrofts were staying at their summer house on the lake—and Gilly was quite a water diver—that is, a skin diver. . . . My idea was that we'd rent a boat, just like a couple of ordinary fishermen, and Gilly would have his skin-diving outfit in the boat. We'd put out and I'd go fishing. He would skin-dive and be at a certain place at a certain time and then we'd have Rosena Andrews drop the money overboard in this coffee can. Gilly would skin-dive under the coffee can, scoop it down under the water, then swim over to the shore line where he'd be undetected and I'd put the boat over in to the shore as though I were looking for fish there. Gilly would climb in and change his clothes and put the skin-diving outfit in the big hamper we had and we'd go on back and turn the boat in and drive away. That way, even if there'd been a squawk to police no one could catch us."

"What happened?" Hastings asked.

"I guess by this time everybody knows what happened," Kelsey said. "We told her to put the money in a coffee can—a red coffee can—and as luck would have it, it just happened there were two red coffee cans. One of them was just an empty can that someone had tossed overboard from a boat after using it for bait, and the other one was the can with the money. Well, it happened that a water skier picked up the can with the money and turned it over to the police, and Gilly grabbed the empty can that had been used as a bait can."

"You discussed the matter with him?"

"After we saw in the paper what had happened, I discussed the matter of his double-cross with him."

"What do you mean by double-cross?"

"About his trying to get three thousand instead of fifteen hundred and holding out the fifteen hundred."

"And what did he say with reference to that?"

"He swore he hadn't made the change in the letter, that someone had double-crossed him and *he* accused *me* of doing it so I could get an extra fifteen hundred."

"All right, then what happened?"

"Well, after we found out we'd picked up the wrong coffee can, Gilly called Rosena and told her that she hadn't followed instructions and she accused him of being a nosy newspaper reporter and hung up. So then he called the mother and she said to meet her down at the float at the Blue Sky Yacht Club and she'd take him out in the yacht and pay the money there and then put him ashore and in that way they could both be sure that nobody was watching, that she thought some private detectives were in on the deal and she wanted privacy just as much as anybody."

"And what time was he to meet her?"

"Seven o'clock on the float at the Blue Sky Yacht Club."

"Do you know whether he did meet her or not?"

"I'm just telling you what I know from what I heard on the telephone and from what Gilly told me. All I know for sure is that Gilly took off for the Blue Sky Yacht Club and that was the last I ever saw of him."

"Cross-examine," Hastings said.

"*How* did he take off for the Blue Sky Yacht Club?" Mason asked.

"I don't know. The last I saw of him was when he was eating dinner in his room. That was about six-thirty. He always went for canned pork and beans in a big way, and my last talk with him was when he was sitting there gulping down canned pork and beans. He said he'd have to leave a little before seven, and that before midnight we'd have our three thousand dollars."

"Then what?"

"Then I went out on some business of my own. After that I went back to the Ajax-Delsey. I also had a room there. I waited and waited for Gilly to come back. When he hadn't come in by midnight, I figured he'd collected the three grand and had taken a powder so he wouldn't have to split with me."

"You knew that Gilly had posed as a friend of Irwin Fordyce?"

"Certainly."

"And under the guise of friendship had got Fordyce to confide in him?"

"Of course."

"And then had deliberately used that information for the purposes of blackmail?"

"Sure," Kelsey said. "I'm no angel. I'm not trying to pose as an angel, and Gilly was in every bit as deep as I was."

"And you had a plan to double-cross Gilly? You planned to force Eve Amory to sign a paper saying the three thousand found in the coffee can was hers, that the whole idea was a scheme for personal publicity for her and that she wanted the police to turn the money back to her, and then you were going to force her to turn it over to you on another blackmailing scheme?"

"That's right. You caught me at it. Gilly was planning on double-crossing me, so I was taking out a little insurance. Gilly wasn't really a partner of mine. He was inexperienced in the blackmail racket so he turned to me to handle the deal. Then he figured on double-crossing me and leaving me holding the sack, so I just decided to take out a little insurance, that's all."

"And you have gone to the district attorney with all this information and used it to gain immunity from prosecution for the blackmail, haven't you?"

"What would you have done?" Kelsey asked.

"I'm asking you the question. Have you done that?"

"Yes."

"And the district attorney gave you money for a haircut, a new suit of clothes and new shoes, so you'd make a good impression in court?"

"Not the district attorney."

"The sheriff?"

"Yes."

"And you have received the promise of immunity from the district attorney?"

"Provided I told the truth on the witness stand."

"And what was his definition of the truth?"

"Well, it had to be a story that there wouldn't be any holes in."

"In other words," Mason said, "if you told a story that would stand up on cross-examination, that was supposed to be the truth. Is that right?"

"Well, something like that."

"If I was able to trip you up on cross-examination and show that you were lying, then you wouldn't have any immunity. Is that it?"

"Well, that's about the size of it, I guess. Of course he didn't express it quite that way, but I was supposed to be telling the truth. If I'm telling the truth, nobody can punch any holes in my story. I'm to tell a story that stands up and then they'll make it easy on me."

"In other words," Mason said, "if your story is good enough to bring about a conviction of the defendant in this case, you won't be prosecuted for blackmail. Is that it?"

"Well, now you're putting your own interpretation on the thing," Kelsey said. "That wasn't exactly the way the D.A. put it up to me and that's not the way I'm going to let you get our understanding into the record. The understanding was that if I told my story and there were no holes in it, and I was telling the truth so it stood up in court just the way I'd told it to the D.A., I didn't have to worry about getting prosecuted for blackmail.

"Now, I'll be perfectly frank with you, Mr. Mason. I'm no angel. I've had trouble and that's why I couldn't answer a question about what my occupation was. I'm not going to commit myself. There isn't any promise of immunity on anything except this one blackmail job. I'm willing to answer all questions about that and I'm going to tell the truth about it, even if it puts me in the position of being something of a heel.

"But you have to remember that I was dealing with a man who really wasn't a partner. He'd just propositioned me to help him put across a blackmail deal, and then he started double-crossing me right from the start. I didn't intend to stand for that."

Mason said, "On the night of the tenth when Gilly was killed, where were you?"

"Now there," Kelsey said, grinning, "I've got a sweet alibi. I was putting the bite on Eve Amory right about the time the murder took place, and after that I drove down to my room and I stayed there all night. I was up until a little after midnight, waiting for Gilly to come in, and when he didn't come in I just decided he'd given me the double-cross, but I didn't care too much because I felt sure I was going to make Eve Amory see things my way.

"Everybody would be sore at her because she'd pulled a fast one to get publicity, but that was no skin off *my* nose. They'd have to turn over the three thousand bucks to her and I'd wind up with all the dough."

"And what became of Irwin Victor Fordyce?" Mason asked.

"Search me. I don't know anything about that deal. All I know is that he was out of stir and he was hot, and he evidently took it on the lam when he found out that Gilly had sold him out and was blackmailing the family. You can see it his way. He felt that sooner or later the blackmail deal would get into the hands of the police, they'd find out what it was all about, and since he was hotter than a three-dollar pistol he decided discretion was the better part of valor and he'd better take it on the lam."

"What do you mean by saying he was hotter than a three-dollar pistol?" Mason asked.

"Just what I said. He had been fingered on a filling station job and the police were looking for him. As soon as he saw that blackmail letter published in the newspaper, he knew that the fat was in the fire and he decided to get out of circulation."

"Did you ever talk it over with him?"

"I never spoke to him in my life," Kelsey said. "I knew him when I saw him because he had a room in the same building where I was staying, but he was Gilly's friend, not mine. He didn't know me from Adam."

"But Gilly knew you."

"Sure, Gilly knew me. I had a reputation for— Well, we're not going into that, but Gilly wanted to put a bite on the Bancrofts and he figured I could tell him how to do it."

"And you told him how to do it?"

"I'm not denying it."

"And you were actually in Gilly's room on the night of the murder."

"That's right. A little before seven o'clock. Sometime between six-thirty and seven."

"And what was Gilly doing?"

"I told you, he was eating his dinner; gulping it down pretty fast because he had to leave. He told me he had everything all fixed, that he was going to get three grand to take the place of the money that had slipped through our fingers and he'd be back with it before midnight.

"Like I told you, he was eating canned beans and bread."

"Coffee?" Mason asked.

"No, he had some milk. He didn't go much for coffee at night. He drank it in the morning I think. I tell you, Mr. Mason, the man wasn't my partner. He was just a— Well, he just came to me to help him out, that's all."

"Then you went out on this expedition of your own and what time did you get back?"

"I don't know. Probably—oh, maybe around nine or nine-thirty."

"And you stayed in your room thereafter?"

"No, I didn't. I went from my room over to Gilly's room—oh, half a dozen times—trying to see if he was in."

"Did you go in?"

"I didn't have any key. He had the door locked. I looked to see if there was a light in the place and then a little after midnight I tapped on the door to see if he'd come in, hadn't gone to my place, and had gone to bed instead. Then about one o'clock in the morning I tried it again. By that time I'd come to the conclusion he'd given me another double-cross, had collected the three grand and had decided to dust out. Well, that was all right with me. I figured I could take care of myself in dealing with a cheap, two-bit crook like Gilly."

"And how did you figure you'd take care of yourself?"

"Like I told you, first I'd make Eve Amory make a statement that the whole thing had been a publicity stunt. That would show she had title to the money. They'd have to give it back to her. I figured that the Bancrofts weren't going to come forward and say it was *their* money, because then they'd have to tell the police all about the blackmail deal and they couldn't afford to do that. So I figured it was all right. Gilly could double-cross me and take the three grand, and I'd double-cross him and get the other three grand and we'd be even. Then I'd take over the blackmail deal and handle it the way it should be done. These were just the first preliminary touches. Before I got done, I was going to put a ten-grand shakedown on the Bancrofts. And then the next time I ran into Gilly I'd make him kick through for the half he'd held out on me."

"What about the half that you'd held out on him?" Mason asked.

"The way I was playing it, that was a separate deal with Eve Amory. That was none of his business."

"And how did you intend to make him give you the half of the three thousand dollars he'd collected from the defendant?"

"Well," Kelsey said slowly, "there are ways and ways. Take my line of business, you have ways of insuring that people who give you a double-cross pay up afterwards."

"What is your line of business?" Mason asked.

Kelsey grinned and said, "Now we're getting back to where we started. I told you I'm not going to talk about my line of business.

Nobody's giving any immunity for anything except this one black-mail deal."

"And you get immunity for that."

"That's right."

"Provided your story stands up," Mason said.

Kelsey said, "You just try to punch a hole in it, Mister. I'm telling you the truth and you just try to find a loose joint in what I have told you. I'm not foolish enough to make a deal with the D.A. and then try to hold out anything and get my neck in a noose. If my story stands up, I get immunity. If it doesn't stand up, I don't. They can say lots of things about Kelsey but they can't say he's too dumb to know which side of the bread has the butter."

"So you have quite an interest in bringing about the conviction of the defendant in this case," Mason said.

"I have quite an interest in being sure I tell the truth," Kelsey said. "I don't care what effect it has. If it ties Mrs. Bancroft up with murder, that's her hard luck. But on the kind of a deal I have, I'm telling the truth and I don't care who gets hurt."

"You know Gilly was going down to the yacht club to meet Mrs. Bancroft?"

"I knew what he told me, yes."

"And when he didn't show up you didn't make any attempt to go down there to the yacht club?"

"I did not. I stayed right in that house and waited for him to come back. I figured I'd give him that much of a chance to shoot square."

"And if he had given you half of the three thousand, would you have given him half of the three thousand you were going to get from Eve Amory?" Mason asked.

"Oh, Your Honor," the district attorney said, "I think this question is argumentative and is entirely outside the field of legitimate cross-examination. I've given the defendant every latitude with this witness because I realize the man is one whose background makes his story open to question.

"If there's any loophole in his story I'm just as anxious to find it out as defense counsel. But certainly, asking him about what he intended to do in the event he'd been successful in blackmailing Miss Amory into giving him a document on which he could subsequently collect the three thousand dollars that was in the hands of the authorities, is hardly within the issues in the present case."

"I think it's argumentative," Judge Hobart ruled. "However, I felt that in a matter of this sort, and dealing with a man of this sort, defense counsel should have every latitude. I think I'll overrule the objection. Answer the question."

"Well," Kelsey said, "I'll put it this way. If Gilly had played square with me, I think I'd have cut him in on that other three grand. Yes, I think I would have. I've got a reputation to sustain—but I was pretty suspicious of Gilly after he'd tried to double-cross me by boosting the ante from fifteen hundred to three thousand and figuring that he'd get the first crack at that coffee can, dip out the extra fifteen hundred and destroy the note— Well, I didn't feel too friendly toward the boy. I just made up my mind he was a chiseler and I'd even up with him on this deal and then I didn't want any more to do with him.

"We have a code of ethics in my business, the same as any other, and the people I'm doing business with are entitled to rely on my reputation—only, I'm not going into my business, Mr. Mason. I'm just talking about this one deal and that's all."

"Thank you," Mason said, smiling. "I think I have no further questions."

District Attorney Hastings said, "I will call as my next witness Dr. Morley Badger, the coroner's physician and autopsy surgeon."

Dr. Badger took the stand.

Mason said, "We will stipulate Dr. Badger's professional qualifications subject to the right of cross-examination."

"Very well. Thank you," the district attorney said.

He turned to the witness. "Dr. Badger, you were called on the eleventh of this month to perform an autopsy?"

"I was."

"On whom did you perform the autopsy?"

"Willmer Gilly; at least, it was a cadaver whose fingerprints have been introduced in evidence as being those of Willmer Gilly."

"What did you find as to the cause of death?"

"A .38-caliber bullet had penetrated the man's heart. It had entered the chest, penetrated the heart, and lodged against the spine."

"What can you say in regard to death?"

"It was instantaneous, as nearly as one can measure those things."

"What about motion after the shot?"

"There would have been no motion after the shot. The bullet not only went through the heart but lodged in the spinal column. The only motion would have been a falling motion due to gravitation. The man fell where he was struck and died where he fell."

"What time did you perform your autopsy?"

"About nine-thirty on the evening of the eleventh."

"How long had the man been dead?"

"Approximately twenty-four hours."

"Can you fix it any closer than that?"

"Medically, I would say the man had died between eight and eleven P.M. of the preceding day; judging from extraneous evidence, I can pinpoint the time of death a little more accurately."

"What do you mean by that?"

"The man had died within approximately an hour and a half to two hours after ingesting a meal of canned pork and beans."

"You may inquire," the district attorney said.

"No questions," Mason said.

"What!" District Attorney Hastings exclaimed in surprise. "No cross-examination?"

"No cross-examination," Mason said.

"If the Court please," Hastings said, "I see it is approaching the hour of the noon adjournment and that is our case. We only need to show in a preliminary hearing of this kind that a crime has been committed and that there is reasonable cause to connect the defendant with the crime. I think we have abundantly established our case."

"It would seem so," Judge Hobart said, "unless, of course, the defendant wishes to put on a defense."

"The defendant would like to have an adjournment," Mason said, "until tomorrow morning."

"Do you intend to put on any defense?" Judge Hobart asked. "It is, of course, unusual in preliminary examinations of this sort and I warn counsel that once a prima facie case has been established, mere conflict of evidence would have virtually no effect on the ruling of the Court. It is this Court's duty to bind a defendant over when there is reasonable cause to believe the defendant has perpetrated a crime. The question of credibility of witnesses in the event of a conflict in the testimony is exclusively within the province of the trial jury."

"I understand, Your Honor," Mason said. "However, the defense is entitled to a reasonable continuance and I would like to have a continuance until tomorrow morning in order to ascertain whether we wish to put on testimony.

"I would also like to make a public statement in court at this time. Inasmuch as the defendant has sustained some damage in the press because of her refusal to make any statement whatever to the investigating officers, and inasmuch as I have been largely responsible for that attitude on the part of the defendant, I would like to announce that immediately following the adjournment of this case there will be a press conference at which the defendant will tell a full and complete story to the newspaper reporters as to exactly what happened on the night of the murder."

"Your Honor!" Hastings shouted, getting to his feet, "this is ridiculous. This is making a travesty of a judicial investigation. The defendant sits tight and makes no statement whatever on the advice of counsel. Then after the prosecution has rested its case, the defendant announces that she will, in effect, give her testimony to the public press."

Judge Hobart said thoughtfully, "I know of no law which prevents the defendant from making a statement to the press at any time the defendant desires, and I certainly know that under the law the defendent does not have to make a statement to investigating officers.

"Under the circumstances, Court will take a recess until tomorrow morning at ten o'clock, at which time this hearing will be renewed. In the meantime the defendant is, of course, remanded to the custody of the sheriff. However, if the defendant desires to make a statement to the press at this time, I see no reason why the sheriff cannot arrange for such an audience here in the courthouse."

Judge Hobart arose and left the bench.

District Attorney Hastings came barging over to Mason's counsel table. "Look here, Mason," he said, "you can't pull a stunt like this!"

"Why can't I?" Mason asked. "You heard what the judge said. It's legal."

"Well, if you're going to have a press conference, I'll be there and I'll ask some questions," Hastings said. "What you're trying to do is to enable the defendant to tell her story without being cross-examined by the prosecution."

"Are you representing a newspaper?" Mason asked.

"You're damned right I am—that is, I will be. I'll have credentials from a newspaper in five minutes."

"Get them," Mason said coldly, "and you'll be entitled to attend the conference."

"And I'll ask some questions that the defendant can't answer—or won't answer."

"If," Mason said, "you are a member of the press, you will be welcome."

The courtroom was seething with excitement. Newspaper photographers, crowding close to Mason's table, took photographs of the irate district attorney and the smiling defense counsel.

Hastings turned to the reporters. "I never heard of anything like this in my life," he said. "It's fantastic! It's ridiculous! It's also suicidal, but it *does* have the effect of building up public sympathy for the defendant. If she was willing to tell her story, why didn't she tell it when the officers were investigating?"

"Because," Mason said, "the officers made a slipshod investigation."

"What do you mean?"

"They didn't send a diver overboard and investigate the bottom of the bay where the boat had come to anchor.

"How do you know what's on the bottom of that bay? You may find evidence that would completely exonerate the defendant. You may find the murder weapon.

"Any reasonably expert investigating technique would call for divers to go overboard at that point, at least to look for the murder weapon. The natural assumption is that the murderer, whoever he was, threw the weapon overboard.

"But what have you done?" Mason went on. "You and the sheriff investigated the case and didn't even mark the spot where the boat was anchored. Now you have forever lost what may be evidence vital to the defendant in the case. Therefore the defendant exercised her right to choose the time when she would tell her story.

"We have always said we would tell the defendant's story at the proper time and in the proper place."

"You just wait," Hastings sputtered. "I'm going to get to a telephone and get the proper press credentials, and if you're so firmly convinced there's evidence around the bottom of the bay where that boat was anchored, why don't you get a diver and go look for it?"

"We don't know where the place is," Mason said. "The boat was towed away under the direction of the sheriff."

Hastings started to say something but was too angry for words. His mouth quivered in a nervous spasm. His face was dead white. His hands were clenched.

Abruptly he turned and strode away in the direction of the telephones.

Mason said to the sheriff, "If you would be so kind, Sheriff, as to arrange for a conference in the law library within say, five minutes, we will have duly accredited members of the press present."

"Now, wait a minute," Sheriff Jewett said, "you're accusing me of incompetence."

"I'm not accusing *you* of incompetence," Mason said. "I have made the statement that your methods of investigation were slipshod."

"Well, it amounts to the same thing."

"All right," Mason said, "if you want it that way, then I'm accusing you of incompetence."

"I don't know whether I care to co-operate with you in connection with a press conference or not," the sheriff said.

"Hey, wait a minute," one of the newspaper reporters said. "What are you trying to do, squelch the biggest story of the year? What the hell are you talking about?"

"I'm running my office," the sheriff said.

One of the other newspaper reporters said, "Sure, you're running your office, Sheriff, but don't forget your friends. We took off our coats and went to work for you at election time and we intend to keep in your corner, but we sure as hell don't want to lose out on a story of this magnitude.

"Do you realize what it means? Here's a wealthy woman accused of murder, with overtones of blackmail in the case. The wire services will eat it up. The metropolitan papers will be screaming for news. It means a big personal income to every reporter here in the courtroom. You can't throttle a story of that sort—moreover, you can't keep the defendant from talking if she wants to talk. All you can do is throw a monkey wrench in the machinery so it will handicap the local reporters who have been in your corner all along, and who will be sidetracked by reporters from the big metropolitan dailies who will come thronging down here by airplane the minute word gets out that Perry Mason is going to let his client talk."

The sheriff thought things over for a moment, then said, "All right. In ten minutes we'll let her make her statement to the press in the law library."

"And we'll see to it that only accredited press representatives are there," Mason said. "Otherwise, my client won't talk."

"The sheriff and his deputies will be there," the sheriff said.

"Of course," Mason smiled. "We want you there."

"Very well, ten minutes from now in the law library," the sheriff said.

Perry Mason said, "Now, Mrs. Bancroft, if you'll just sit down here behind this table facing the representatives of the press, I'm going to ask you to tell your story."

Bancroft tugged at Mason's sleeve. "Mason," he said in a whisper, "do you think this is wise? To me it seems suicidal."

"I think it's wise," Mason said. "It may be suidical, but it's a calculated risk."

The lawyer turned to Mrs. Bancroft. "Now, go right ahead, Mrs. Bancroft. I'm going to ask you a few preliminary questions first. . . . You were being blackmailed by Gilly?"

"Yes. I had paid him the sum of one thousand dollars."

"When?"

"About the eighth, I think it was."

"I'm going to ask you to avoid telling what the blackmail was about, but I am going to ask you this. Was it because of anything you had done?"

"No."

"It was because of some information which he threatened to release, which you felt would affect the happiness of other people?"

"That's right."

"Now then, after you had paid Gilly this money, when did you next see him?"

"Aboard my yacht, the *Jinesa*, on the tenth."

"You had been aboard the yacht previously with someone else?"

"Yes."

"Who?"

"With Irwin Victor Fordyce."

"You had taken him down to the yacht?"

"Yes."

"And he was the young man that Drew Kirby had seen with you that night?"

"Oh now, just a minute, just a minute," Robley Hastings interposed. "I'm here representing the press but I don't like to have you lead the witness into all these statements. You couldn't do it in court and I don't think you should do it here.

"I now see why you have staged this elaborate press interview. It's so you can put words in the witness's mouth."

Mason said, "You're here as a representative of the press, not as the district attorney. I'm conducting this interview in my own way. Now sit down and shut up."

"As a representative of the press I don't have to either sit down or shut up," Hastings said.

"All right," Mason said, "I'm running the show. I'm giving the conditions under which Mrs. Bancroft will tell her story. How about it, gentlemen, do you want her to go ahead and tell it my way, or do you want to have the interview called off because the district attorney, who is here masquerading as a representative of the press, thinks that my questions are irregular?"

A chorus of voices said, "No! No! Handle it your way. We want the story. We'd like to question her afterwards."

"You can question her all you want afterwards," Mason said, "but she's going to tell her story under conditions which are fair to her. And she isn't going to be browbeaten by the district attorney, nor am I going to be browbeaten by him."

"Let her go ahead," one of the reporters said.

"I still protest," Hastings said. "I—"

"Shut up, Hastings!" one of the newspaper reporters interrupted "You keep on talking and you're going to kill a hell of a good story. Now shut up!"

"How *dare* you talk to me that way?" Hastings asked.

"I dare to talk to you that way because I'm a working newspaper man. I'm a representative of an out-of-town newspaper but still in the county. My rag fought against you when you were running for office and we're going to fight against you when you run for office again. In the meantime you're not going to kill a good story with a lot of courtroom technicalities."

Hastings started to say something, then subsided into silence.

"Now then, go on, tell us what happened," Mason said to Mrs

Bancroft. "What were you trying to do with Fordyce? Why did you take him down to the yacht club?"

"Because I wanted him to take our yacht and go to Catalina in it."

"Why?"

"I wanted him where Gilly couldn't find him."

"And why did you want him where Gilly couldn't find him?"

"Because I thought Gilly had—well, I thought Gilly wasn't to be trusted. I thought Gilly would try to find him and get information from him and use that information against me and against people I care for."

"All right, what happened?" Mason said.

"I wanted to get some money for him. I didn't have very much money in my purse, so I went to some friends who I knew kept cash on hand. I'm not going to mention their names but they cashed a three-thousand-dollar check for me. They don't want to be brought into this and it's very understandable why they don't."

"Why don't they?" Mason asked.

"Because they keep several thousand dollars in cash in the house all the time and if that word got around it would simply make them a target for holdups."

"That's very understandable," Mason said. "Now, what happened? You got the money and rowed back to the boat. What happened when you got aboard?"

"The motor was running, idling. I tied up the dinghy and boarded the boat and went down to the cabin. Then I saw this figure up in the bow, pulling in the anchor chain. I thought that it was Fordyce. I switched on a light in the cabin. The man at the bow of the boat saw the light, made a half-hitch of the anchor chain around the bitt in the bow of the boat, turned and came back to the cabin.

"Before he entered the cabin he had engaged the clutch and the boat was running forward at slow speed, dragging an undetermined amount of anchor chain."

"Go ahead," Mason said.

"It was then I realized that this man was not Fordyce, but was Gilly. I asked him where Fordyce was, I asked him what he had done with Fordyce, and he made no answer."

"What was the weather?" Mason asked.

"There was a heavy fog."

"And the boat was running in this fog?"

"Yes."

"Apparently on any course, or just aimlessly?"

"Apparently on some course which this man had set."

"What happened?"

"I became frightened. I started backing up and he moved slowly toward me. I asked him again where Fordyce was and he started for me with his hands outstretched as though he intended to choke me."

"Now, that's a conclusion," Hastings said. "You don't know that he intended to choke you."

"Shut up!" the out-of-town reporter said. "We'll question her after she gives her story."

Mrs. Bancroft said, "Well, he certainly looked as though he intended to choke me. He had his hands outstretched and his attitude was menacing in the extreme."

"What did you do?" Mason asked.

She said, "I was frightened stiff. Then I remembered that I had a gun in my purse."

"What gun?"

"My husband's gun."

"Where did you get that?"

"From a dresser by the side of the bed. The gun was always kept in a drawer in that dresser."

"And what did you do with it?"

"I pulled it out and pointed it at him and said he was to stop."

"Was the gun cocked?"

"It was a six-shooter and I cocked it. I knew enough to do that."

"How did you know enough to do that?"

"Because my husband wanted me to know how to shoot in case of necessity. When we were up at the mountain cabin he always had me shoot several shots at a target there."

"With this gun?"

"With this same gun."

"All right," Mason said, "what happened?"

"The man hesitated a moment, then he started for me again and I was paralyzed with fright.

"At that particular moment the dragging anchor struck on the bottom and brought the boat to an abrupt halt; that is, it gave the boat a momentary jar and—I have no conscious recollection of pulling the trigger, but the jar caused me to lose my balance and I did pull the trigger."

"And what happened?"

"I shot him."

"Where?"

"Right in the chest."

"How do you know?"

"Because that's where the gun was pointed when it went off and he fell forward."

"What did you do?"

"Even while he was falling I was running. I dashed to the side of the boat and jumped overboard."

"Why did you jump overboard?"

"Because I was frightened."

"What were you frightened of?"

"Of Willmer Gilly."

"But if you had just shot him and he was dead, why were you frightened of him?"

"I . . . I don't know. I guess I . . . I guess at the time I wasn't certain I had killed him. I just wanted to get off the boat."

"What happened to the gun?"

"I'm not certain. I was fumbling, trying to get it back in the purse when I jumped. I think I heard it hit the deck and then splash into the water."

"And where was the purse?"

"On my arm. That is, I had the strap around my wrist."

"You don't know that you took the gun overboard with you?"

"I think I did. I tell you, I think I remember hearing it hit on the deck and then splash."

"And your purse?"

"I know I lost my purse when I went overboard because it was on my wrist when I jumped and it slid off."

"What did you do then?"

"I went in over my head and started swimming and then of course tried to get my bearings. Then I saw a light on the shore and started for shore."

"How far did you swim?"

"Only a few strokes, and then I thought the water might be shallow and put my feet down and sure enough the water wasn't much over my waist. I was able to wade along on the bottom."

"And then what did you do?"

"I waded ashore."

"Did you know where you were when you got ashore?"

"I knew where I was before I got ashore."

"How?"

"There was a wharf near the boat and I recognized it."

"What kind of a wharf?"

"It was a wharf where they sell oil and gasoline. It is the wharf that's only about two or three hundred yards from the parking station at the yacht club."

"Is it the first gasoline wharf to the north of the yacht club?"

"Yes."

"How close was the boat to that?"

"Well, Mr. Mason, I guess, as I think back on it, the tide was coming in, and after the anchor struck something solid and held, the boat started to swing with the incoming tide, and it had swung toward the wharf—I don't think I was over thirty or forty feet from the wharf when I went in the water. I was within twenty or thirty feet of the wharf when I recognized it. By that time I was just wading ashore."

"And what did you do?"

"I walked to the parking lot. I keep the keys to my automobile under the floor mat because sometimes I've forgotten my purse or lost the car keys, so I got the car keys out from under the mat and started the car."

"Then what did you do?"

"I drove home, I got out of my wet clothes and—well, I told my husband what had happened."

"And what did he do?"

"He said that I was completely hysterical, that it would be a bad thing for me to get in touch with the police at that time, particularly until we knew what had happened, that he was going to go down and look at the boat and see if I had actually killed Gilly and if so he would notify the police.

"He prevailed on me to take some pills. They were very strong pills that had been given him as a sedative because of very painful symptoms which sometimes came on him unexpectedly in the middle of the night. He had those pills in reserve. And he gave me a double dose to quiet me."

"And what happened?"

"I was nervous for a while, then the pills began to take effect. I felt deliciously warm and relaxed, and the next thing I knew it was just about daylight and my husband was standing over me and said, 'Phyllis, take this water and swallow this pill.'"

"What did you do?"

"I woke up enough to take another pill."

Mason turned to the newspapermen. "There you are, gentlemen," Mason said. "There's the story. Now, if you have a brief period of questioning, my client will try to answer your questions."

One of the newspapermen said, "What time was this; that is, when you fired the shot?"

Mrs. Bancroft faced him frankly. "I think the coroner was probably right as to the time of death," she said. "It was right around nine o'clock."

"Do you mean to tell me you hadn't seen Gilly prior to that time on that day?" Hastings asked.

"I had not seen him. I was trying to avoid him. It came as a distinct surprise to me to find him aboard the yacht."

"A likely story," Hastings said.

"Suppose you let us do the talking," the out-of-town newspaperman said. "I want to get the facts of this story. Can you tell us something about the reason you wanted this man, Fordyce, to live aboard your boat, Mrs. Bancroft?"

She said, "Fordyce was— Well, he was in a position where— No, I'm afraid I can't tell you that without disclosing something I don't want to disclose."

"Did the blackmail have something to do with Fordyce?"

"I'd prefer not to answer that question."

"You'd paid him a thousand dollars—this man, Gilly?"

"Yes."

"And your daughter, Rosena, had paid three thousand dollars?"

"My daughter had not confided in me exactly what had happened, but I do happen to know that she also was being blackmailed."

"Over the same thing?"

"Yes."

"Then this subject of blackmail was something that affected her happiness as well as your own?"

"I'd prefer not to answer that."

One of the other newspapermen said, "Do you know where your husband went after you went to sleep?"

"No."

"He told you he was going down to the boat?"

"Yes."

"Did you have any talk with him afterwards about whether he had been aboard the boat?"

"Yes. He said he drove down and couldn't find the boat. He said that he walked out on the wharf. There was a thick pea-soup fog but I had told him that with the incoming tide the boat would be close enough to the wharf so he could see it. In fact, it would have been within . . . oh, I think ten or fifteen feet of the wharf by the time the tide had swung it around on the anchor."

"He said he couldn't see it?"

"Yes."

"He admitted to you, however, that he went down to the bay after you became unconscious."

"Yes."

"And tried to find the boat?"

"Yes."

"What time was that, that he went down?" Hastings asked.

"I don't know, but I do know that it was around ten o'clock when I got home and got out of my wet clothes, and after I had told him my story—I guess it must have been ten-thirty or quarter of eleven before I went to sleep."

"And your husband was with you until you went to sleep?"

"Yes."

"Then," Hastings said to the newsmen, "since the time of death was fixed at around nine o'clock it would have been impossible for her husband to have taken over and been the one who fired the fatal shot, which I think is the idea Perry Mason is trying to implant in your minds."

The newspapermen looked at each other.

One of the men said, "I have some more questions but they can keep. This story won't keep. I want to get it on the wires before I'm scooped."

"You said it," one of the other men said. "Let's go."

They went pell-mell out of the law library, leaving Hastings, the district attorney, behind.

"I have a few more questions," Hastings said.

"Don't you want to get your story on the wire?" Mason asked, smiling.

"No," Hastings said, "not yet. I want to get some more information."

Mason smiled at him and said, "Under the circumstances, Mr. Hastings, I think your devotion to your occupation as district attorney of this county is more deep-seated, loyal and sincere than your devotion to the paper which has temporarily given you a press card so that you could attend this conference.

"I wish to inform you that the interrogation period is over and Mrs. Bancroft is not going to answer any more questions."

Hastings turned to Bancroft and said, "How about you? You went down to the wharf and—"

"Don't misunderstand us," Mason said. "This is a press conference to hear the story of Mrs. Bancroft. Her husband is not making any statement."

Hastings said, "This is the same old run-around. You're going to try to make it appear that her husband went down to the wharf, that there were two guns, that he was the one who shot Gilly and you'll try to get Mrs. Bancroft off and then when we try the husband you'll make it appear that Mrs. Bancroft was the one who fired the shot. As far as I'm concerned, your story crucifies her right now.

"And if she wants to claim self-defense, just let her try and explain why she didn't notify the police right away."

"Because," Mason said, "she didn't want to expose the matter which had been used as a means of blackmail. She didn't want to have the police interrogating her about the subject of blackmail and about why she had taken Fordyce down to the yacht in the first place."

Hastings said, "Let her tell that story on the witness stand where I've got an opportunity to cross-examine her and I'll rip her story to shreds—and when she tries to tell that story, don't think the

Court will let you stand around and put words in her mouth. She'll tell it according to the rules of evidence, the same as any other witness.

"As far as I'm concerned, this thing has been just a dress rehearsal and an attempt on your part to influence the press into giving her a sympathetic sob-sister background.

"I challenge you to put her on the witness stand tomorrow and let her tell that same story."

"You prepare your case and I'll prepare mine," Mason said. "The press conference is over."

21

Sheriff Jewett said, "In view of your client's statement, Mr. Mason, I don't see why you accused me of incompetent investigative technique in that I failed to mark the location of the yacht where we recovered it. Quite evidently the yacht had drifted with the rising tide down the bay and had come to rest there."

"The point is," Mason said, "that you don't know what went overboard from that yacht. You don't know *what* evidence might have been thrown overboard."

"What makes you think any evidence was?"

"I think it was," Mason said. "I think something very significant was thrown overboard. I also think that in the best police procedure any investigation worthy of the name would have marked the exact location of that yacht and had divers explore the bottom."

"I don't know what you're getting at," the sheriff said.

"You'll find out before I rest my case," Mason told him.

The sheriff said, "All right, I'll tell you the same thing you told the district attorney. You run your business and I'll run mine."

"Thank you," Mason said, smiling. "As far as I'm concerned the press conference is over. I'll see you tomorrow, Mrs. Bancroft, and in the meantime don't answer any more questions. Just say that you'll tell your story at the proper time and in the proper place. From now on, keep your own counsel. Don't tell anybody anything."

Mason stalked out of the room.

Della Street said, "Why didn't you show the sheriff up by proving that two typewriters had been used on that note?"

Mason smiled at her. "It won't help our case to get the sheriff confused, but it will help our case to keep the blackmailers confused."

"Why? One of them is dead."

"Do you know that there were only two?" Mason asked.

She thought over his question for a few seconds. "No," she admitted at length.

"Exactly," Mason said, and then, after a pause, "Let's eat."

22

It was four o'clock when Mason got Paul Drake on the phone.

"You down there at the bay, Paul?"

"I'm down here."

"What's the weather?"

"Foggy again."

"Damn it," Mason said, "I was hoping the fog would lift."

"Well, it *may* be lifting. It looks as though it's getting a little lighter."

"You're camped down there by that wharf?"

"Hell, I'm on the wharf," Drake said. "I've got a set of white coveralls with the name of an oil company all over the back and I'm ostensibly waiting for boats to come in to be refueled."

"All right, keep your eyes open," Mason said.

"What am I looking for?"

"Divers," Mason told him. "I think before the afternoon is over you'll find the district attorney and the sheriff down there with some divers. I've got the sheriff worried. He thinks that maybe he should have explored the bottom of the bay around where the yacht was found, and I'm positive the district attorney will try to disprove Mrs. Bancroft's testimony by sending a diver down to look over the place where she says she jumped overboard. I think he's convinced the actual murder took place out where the yacht was found."

"All right, I'll stick on the job," Drake said.

"And when any divers come along I'll want to know," Mason told him. "You have a phone there?"

"Right here on the wharf," Drake said. "I'm sitting here inside the little cabin at the end of the wharf and looking out over the bay right now."

"All right," Mason said, "keep looking."

"How long do I stay here?"

"Have someone bring your meals," Mason told him. "Get a relief, if you have to, but I'd prefer to have you on the job personally."

"It's colder than hell with this fog," Drake said. "I came down here with just a business suit. I've got these white coveralls over it but they're not sufficient."

"Try running and jumping up and down," Mason told him. "Try thumping your hands against your thighs. That will keep the circulation going. Make your arms go up and down. Pretend you're a sea gull, trying to fly."

"Go jump in the lake," Drake told him. "It's easy for you to sit up there in a heated office with the temperature regulated by a thermostat and tell me what to do to keep warm."

Mason chuckled. "Just stay on the job, Paul. I've been a big help already, you're mad enough now to keep warm for an hour."

23

It was a little after five o'clock when Drake called Mason.

"Okay, Perry," he said, "we've got action down here."

"You're at the wharf?"

"Yes."

"How's the weather?"

"It's clear."

"Cold?"

"Not as bad as it was when the fog was in."

"What's the action?"

"The sheriff, the district attorney, a couple of deputies and a diver."

"What are they doing?"

"Just standing around, waiting for the diver— Oh, oh, here comes the diver now. He has something in his hand."

"Can you see what it is?" Mason asked.

"No, the diver has motioned to the sheriff and the district attorney and he's going ashore with it. He isn't coming out here to the wharf."

"Keep an eye on things," Mason said. "Just hang onto the phone and let me know what's happening."

"All right. They're in a huddle now," Drake said, "and it's quite a huddle. . . . Here's the diver going back. He's swimming under water. You can get an idea of where he is by the air bubbles."

"You don't have any idea what it was he found?"

"No."

"Couldn't get any glimpse of it?"

"No."

"Think it's the purse?"

"Probably. It was right out there where the purse was—right where— Hey, wait a minute, Perry. He's back again. There are two things. They're positively jubilant. The district attorney is patting the diver on the back."

Mason said, "Take off your coveralls and go to dinner, Paul. Your shift is over."

24

Judge Hobart said, "Case of the People versus Phyllis Bancroft. This is the time heretofore fixed to resume the hearing and hear the defendant's case. Are you ready, gentlemen?"

"Just a moment," Hastings said. "If the Court please, we announced yesterday that we were going to rest our case but with the indulgence of the Court I would like to ask a few more questions to clear up certain matters which have been in doubt and remove certain criticisms which have been directed toward the law enforcement agencies of the county in a press conference—"

"The Court is not concerned with criticisms or with press conferences," Judge Hobart interrupted. "If you wish to put on other evidence after having rested your case, the Court will consider this a motion to reopen the case. Is there any objection from the defense?"

"None whatever," Mason said.

Hastings said triumphantly, "Call Sheriff Jewett to the stand.

"You have already been sworn, Sheriff. There is no need for you to take the oath again. Just be seated.

"Now, Sheriff, directing your attention to a so-called press conference which occurred yesterday afternoon, did you hear the defendant make any statement at that press conference?"

"I did."

"Did that statement have any reference to the defendant's action on the night of the tenth?"

"It did."

"What did she say, as nearly as you can recall, about the shooting?"

"She said that she had a gun in her purse, that she took the gun from her purse and killed Willmer Gilly, that she then jumped overboard from the yacht on which the killing took place, that at that time she was carrying a purse which she dropped—she thought she dropped it after she struck the water and she was holding the gun which she dropped as she went overboard. She said she thought she heard it hit the deck and then splash in the water."

"Now then," Hastings said, "after hearing that story, did you go to the place where she had indicated the shooting took place at the harbor?"

"I did."

"Did you have anyone with you?"

"I did. I had a trained diver."

"And what did this diver do under your direction?"

"He explored the bottom of the bay."

"What did he find, if anything?"

"He found a woman's purse."

"I show you a woman's purse," Hastings said, "which contains some identification cards and a driving license, rather water-soaked but still legible, in the name of Phyllis Bancroft, and ask you if you have seen this before?"

"I have. That is the purse which the diver handed me."

"We ask that that be introduced as an appropriate exhibit," Hastings said.

Judge Hobart frowned thoughtfully as he looked at Mason. "Are there any objections?"

"None whatever, Your Honor."

"Now then, did the diver uncover anything else?"

"He did."

"What?"

"A gun."

"Can you describe that gun?"

"Yes, sir. That was a .38-caliber Smith and Wesson six-shooting revolver, No. 133347. It had five loaded shells in it and one exploded cartridge, and an examination of the records showed the gun had been purchased by Harlow Bissinger Bancroft, the husband of the defendant."

"Did you make any ballistic tests with that gun?"

"I did, yes, sir."

"And make any comparison of the test bullets fired from that gun, with the fatal bullet?"

"Yes, sir."

"What was the result?"

"The tests showed this revolver was the weapon which fired the fatal bullet."

"Now then," Hastings went on, "in the course of the press conference there were some criticisms which were leveled at your office for not having marked the exact location where the boat was discovered on the afternoon of the eleventh, and not having explored the bottom near the place where the boat was found. Did you make any attempt subsequently to locate the exact place where that boat was found?"

"I did. Yes. sir."

"And what was the result with reference to being able to locate the exact spot where the boat had been anchored?"

"I found the exact spot."

"How?"

"By consulting a helicopter pilot who had first discovered the boat and who had taken a photograph showing the boat with reference to landmarks on the shore line which enabled us to pinpoint the location."

"Did you send a diver down to that location?"

"Yes, sir."

"What, if anything, did he discover?"

"Absolutely nothing."

"Now then," Hastings said triumphantly to Mason, "you may cross-examine."

Mason said, "Sheriff, as I understand it, this diver found the purse and the gun at the exact location Mrs. Bancroft had told you it would be, or rather at the exact location she told you the articles should be found."

"Yes, sir."

"Thereby corroborating her story?"

The sheriff crossed his legs and uncrossed them, smiled and said, "Well, it depends on what you mean by corroboration. It's like the hunter who tells you that he stood by an oak tree and shot a deer a thousand yards away with one shot and if you want corroboration he can take you to the oak tree."

Spectators tittered in the courtroom.

Judge Hobart said coldly, "There is no cause for levity, and no reason to be facetious, Sheriff."

"I beg the Court's pardon. I was not trying to be facetious. I was asked if the finding of the articles didn't corroborate the defendant's story and I tried to answer as best I could. There was no corroboration of her story, no, sir—not to that part of her story as to what had happened aboard the yacht. The finding of the articles was equally consistent with willful, premeditated murder."

"Now, you say that you have a photograph taken by the pilot of the helicopter?"

"Yes, sir."

"Showing the location where the boat was discovered?"

"Yes, sir."

"Will you produce that photograph, please?"

The sheriff extended his hand and District Attorney Hastings handed him an eight-by-ten photograph.

"This is the photograph," the sheriff said. "That is, it's an enlargement that shows the boat and you can see where we have drawn cross-lines on the photograph, tying in with certain landmarks which are unmistakable."

"Very well," Mason said. "Now, have you compared that photograph and the position of the yacht with the geodetic survey chart which I had introduced in evidence?"

"I haven't, but I can."

"Please do so, and tell us the depth of the water at that point."

The sheriff turned to the clerk who fumbled through papers and then produced the chart which Mason had had introduced in evidence earlier in the hearing.

After some computation and checking, the sheriff said, "As nearly as I can tell, the depth of the water at that point at mean low tide is ten feet."

"You don't know how much anchor chain was out on the boat when you found it?"

"Yes, sir. I do. There was approximately fifteen feet of anchor chain."

"But when you found the boat and when this photograph was taken," Mason said, "the boat was swinging around the anchor on an outgoing tide. A few hours earlier the boat must have been swinging around on an incoming tide, and with fifteen feet of anchor chain out the boat would have swung in quite an arc."

"I think the diver made allowances for that."

"You say you think he did."

"I instructed him to cover the bottom all around there."

Mason said, "At this time, if the Court please, I move to strike out all statements made by this witness as to what the diver did, what the diver saw and what the diver recovered, because those remarks represent hearsay and are not the best evidence."

"Oh, if the Court please," Hastings said, "we can connect these matters up. We have the diver here in court. I hadn't intended to call him but I can if it becomes necessary."

"Then you had better call him," Mason said, "because I will state that if I have an opportunity to cross-examine this diver I will withdraw my motion. Otherwise I will ask to have all of this evidence stricken."

"Very well," Hastings said, "you may step down, Sheriff, and I will call Fremont L. Dibble to the stand."

Dibble took the oath, qualified himself as the diver who had been employed by the sheriff and the district attorney to search the bottom of the bay in certain definite localities.

"Directing your attention to the first location which was near a fueling wharf immediately to the north of the yacht club, what did you find on the bottom?"

"I found a woman's purse and a gun."

"I show you this woman's purse which has been introduced in evidence and ask you if that is the purse you found."

"Yes, sir."

"I show you a gun and ask you if that is the gun you found."

"Yes, sir."

"Cross-examine," Hastings snapped.

"Is this purse in the same condition as when you found it?" Mason asked.

The witness looked it over carefully. "Yes, sir."

"The contents are the same?"

"Yes, sir."

"There was no money in the purse when you found it?"

"Yes, sir, there was. There's a coin purse in there containing three twenty-dollar bills, two ten-dollar bills, a five-dollar bill, three one-dollar bills and some small change."

"That was in the purse when you found it?"

"Yes, sir."

"No other money?"

"No other money. No, sir."

"The gun is in the same condition as when you found it?"

"Yes, sir."

"Where was the gun with reference to the purse?"

"The gun was lying about . . . oh, twenty or thirty feet away, I would say."

Mason said, "Now, the district attorney didn't ask you, but apparently you are the diver who subsequently went to the point which I am now indicating on the coast geodetic chart by a penciled circle which I will mark with the word 'yacht'. Is that correct?"

"Yes, sir."

"And you searched the bottom there?"

"Yes, sir."

"And found nothing?"

"That is right."

"Absolutely nothing?"

"Oh," the witness said, "there was an old bait can that had been used for bait and thrown overboard. That, however, was about a hundred feet from the boat; that is, the place where the boat was found."

"But if the boat had been swinging around with the tide it would have been nearer to the boat at high tide?"

The witness thought for a moment and said, "Yes, I believe so."

"How did you know it was a bait can?" Mason asked.

The witness smiled and said, "In water of that depth the illumination is very good. I was able to read the label on the can. It had contained canned beans and was empty. Therefore, I called it an old bait can."

"What kind of a label?"

"Oh, just an ordinary label, a piece of paper that had been circled around the can and pasted."

"You described it as an *old* bait can?"

"Well," the witness said, smiling, "I didn't see anyone fishing and I judged it had been there for some time."

"With the label still on it?" Mason asked.

The witness frowned thoughtfully and said, "Well, come to think of it, since the label was still on it I guess I'd better describe it as just a bait can rather than an *old* bait can. It is a question of how old is old."

The witness smiled at the district attorney.

"Thank you," Mason said, "that's all."

"Now, if the Court please," Mason said, "in view of this evidence I would like to ask one or two more questions on cross-examination of the prosecution's witness, Stilson L. Kelsey."

"I think you are entitled to recross-examine any witness you care to in view of the introduction of this new evidence after the prosecution had closed its case," Judge Hobart said. "Mr. Kelsey, come forward."

Kelsey, with something of a swagger this time, took his position on the stand.

Mason said, "Mr. Kelsey, you were not at the press conference yesterday when the defendant told her story."

"No, sir."

"But you did hear what that story was?"

"I did."

"And did you then hurriedly make a trip to the beach with a diving outfit, go to the place the defendant had described, dive under water, there find the purse belonging to the defendant and which contained some three thousand dollars in fifty and hundred-dollar bills, which you appropriated, and then, in order to plant evidence which would clinch the case against the defendant, drop the murder gun near the place where the purse was lying?"

"What!" Kelsey exclaimed. "Why, I—"

"Oh, Your Honor," Hastings interposed, "this is improper cross-examination. This is completely incompetent. This witness is not on trial."

"He will be on trial," Mason said, "because I propose to show that before the defendant told her story I had a diver carefully explore the bottom of the bay at this point, that at that time the defendant's purse was lying there with three thousand dollars in it; that I had the diver take out the three thousand dollars and substitute three thousand dollars which I had drawn from a bank and on which I had kept the numbers of the bills; that at that time there was no gun anywhere near the location of the purse.

"Now then, someone hurriedly went to the spot, removed the three thousand dollars from the purse and put the murder weapon where it would be found.

"That person must have been the murderer—the person who was Gilly's partner, who joined him on the yacht sometime after the defendant had left, who had a boat which he tied to the yacht, who stayed with the yacht while the tide rose and the boat drifted to another part of the bay, who sat with Gilly while he made a meal of canned beans which they took from the boat's stock of provisions; that they tossed the bean can overboard, that they then got in an argument, that this person accused Gilly of double-crossing him on the reward, and shot Gilly with the weapon which Mrs. Bancroft had dropped to the deck of the boat when she jumped overboard.

"Then this person left the body on the yacht, after searching it for money and finding none.

"The murderer then rowed back to shore and—"

"Now, wait a minute," Kelsey said, "you can't accuse me of that because a detective was shadowing me. He followed me all the way from my interview with Eve Amory to the Ajax-Delsey Apartments."

Mason smiled. "So you knew you were being followed?"

"Of course."

"And," Mason said, "what was to prevent you, knowing that you were being followed and the detective was shadowing the front of the Ajax-Delsey Apartments, from slipping out the back way, borrowing a car which you found parked there, and going to the harbor?"

"You can't prove anything of the sort," Kelsey said.

"Yes I can," Mason said, "because those bills which I had placed in Mrs. Bancroft's purse were furnished me by a bank long after the murder had been committed, and the bank has the numbers of those bills, and unless I'm very mistaken you have that three thousand dollars in bills either in your pocket now or concealed somewhere in your room or in your automobile, and I intend to get a search warrant and—"

For one long, trapped moment Kelsey surveyed Mason, sized up the situation, then suddenly and before anyone could stop him, bolted from the witness stand and through the door to the judge's chambers.

After the first numbing shock of surprise the sheriff went pell-mell in pursuit.

Mason turned and grinned at Bancroft.

From a distant corridor came the sound of a voice shouting, "Halt or I'll shoot!"

Two shots were fired in quick succession.

A few minutes later the sheriff returned to court, leading a handcuffed Kelsey.

"Now then, if the Court please," Mason said, "I think if the sheriff will search his prisoner he will find a roll of bills in the prisoner's pocket and that the numbers on those bills will coincide with the list furnished me by the bank, and which I now hand to the sheriff.

"Kelsey thought that Gilly had double-crossed him in connection with the three thousand dollars. After hearing Gilly's story on the yacht he thought that Gilly had again double-crossed him in that Mrs. Bancroft had given him a large sum of money before she had pulled the gun on him.

"The Court will remember that the jar of the yacht running around was sufficient to throw Mrs. Bancroft off balance and cause her to pull the trigger of the gun. It is only natural to assume that Gilly was also thrown off balance, and after having been shot at, had the presence of mind to lie still so that he wouldn't be shot at again.

"Kelsey accused Gilly of double-crossing him. He had the gun, which had not fallen overboard at all but had remained where it had dropped on the deck. He used that gun to kill Gilly in cold blood, and then searched him for the money which he thought Gilly would have. He was disappointed and surprised to find that Gilly didn't have it.

"He then left the yacht, rowed ashore, got in the car he had borrowed or stolen, returned to the back door of the Ajax-Delsey Apartments, went to Gilly's apartment and there carefully fabricated the evidence which indicated Gilly's last meal had been consumed in the apartment *before* he went to the yacht club. In that way he was able to cause the coroner's office to believe death had occurred several hours earlier."

Judge Hobart looked at the cringing Kelsey, said to the sheriff, "Search that man. Let's see if he has bills in his possession, the numbers of which coincide with this list which Mr. Mason has just handed me."

25

Ten minutes later when Judge Hobart, assisted by the district attorney, had carefully checked the numbers of the bills found in Kelsey's wallet, Judge Hobart said, "These numbers check, Mr. Mason. I take it, Mr. Hastings, that a motion to dismiss the case against Mrs. Bancroft is in order."

"I make that motion now," Hastings said somewhat sheepishly.

"Now, I want to say something," Kelsey said.

"Anything you say can be used against you," Judge Hobart said. "You don't have to make any statement. If you do make any statement it is to be made freely and voluntarily and can be used against you."

"I know what the score is," Kelsey said wearily. "I just want to state that Mr. Mason had it all doped out except one thing. I actually shot Gilly in self-defense. I accused him of cheating, accused him of lying and accused him of having made a shake-down that I knew nothing about.

"He denied the accusation and I told him I intended to search him. I started for him and he grabbed a knife, which he had evidently taken from the galley, and came for me. I shot him."

"Then what did you do?" Judge Hobart asked.

"I searched him for money. I didn't find as much as I thought I was going to find but I did find what was left of the thousand dollars that he had secured from Mrs. Bancroft earlier. He was a complete double-crosser and a heel and when he knew I was going to discover what he had done he tried to kill me."

"What did you do with the gun?" Judge Hobart asked.

"I took that gun and concealed it where it wouldn't be found. Later on when I learned the story Mrs. Bancroft had told the press I reloaded one chamber in that gun and tossed away the empty cartridge. I got a skin diver's outfit, went down, located the purse, took out the money, planted the gun near the purse. I felt that under the circumstances I was entitled to that money. It had been my brains that had enabled Gilly to cash in on the idea."

Judge Hobart turned to Mason. "What happened to the bullet that Mrs. Bancroft fired?"

"There was only one thing that could have happened to it," Mason said. "It missed Gilly when he stumbled forward, probably missing him by a scant half-inch, went past his head and out through the open door of the cabin. Remember that Gilly had been raising the anchor, that he had the motor started, that he threw the clutch into gear as he started back and then entered the cabin. The side door must have been open. The bullet Mrs. Bancroft fired must have gone through that door."

Judge Hobart frowned thoughtfully. "This has been a most interesting and a most significant case," he said. "The defendant is to be congratulated upon the strategy by which her counsel trapped the real murderer.

"Now may I ask, as a matter of information, whether it is true that the witness, Drew Kirby, was mistaken as to the identity of the man who was with Mrs. Bancroft earlier on the evening of the tenth?"

"He was mistaken," Mason said, "and that person was actually Irwin Victor Fordyce."

"And what has happened to Fordyce?" Judge Hobart asked.

"He was either murdered," Mason said, "or he has seen fit to disappear in order to keep himself out of circulation."

Harlow Bancroft arose. "May I make a statement, if the Court please?"

"Go ahead," Judge Hobart said.

"I think Irwin Fordyce disappeared because he knew the police were looking for him in connection with a service station holdup. I think he felt that he had two strikes against him because of a previous conviction.

"I want to take this opportunity to state publicly that we can all of us make mistakes. I have made my own mistakes. At one time in my irresponsible youth, I stole an automobile and served a term in the penitentiary for stealing that automobile. I have since lived that down and tried to make good. I want to state publicly here and now that if Irwin Fordyce will surrender himself I will see to it that he has a fair trial and the best legal brains that money can buy. I will pay Mr. Mason's fee to defend him, and if he is guilty of the service station holdup, he has to pay the penalty. If he isn't guilty of the service station holdup, I am going to see that he is acquitted and if he is acquitted I am going to see that he has a responsible position in one of my companies and that he has an opportunity to work up."

Newspaper photographers crowded forward with flashguns blazing intermittently.

Judge Hobart smiled slightly and said, "I am glad you made that statement, Mr. Bancroft. That was spoken like a man and I feel certain that in the years to come you will be glad you have said what you have just stated.

"And as far as your comments about the best legal brains that money can buy, I think the outcome of this case speaks for itself.

"The defendant is released from custody. Mr. Kelsey is in the hands of the sheriff. The Court will impound this money found on him as evidence and court is now adjourned."

26

Mason, Della Street, Paul Drake, Harlow Bancroft, Phyllis Bancroft and Rosena Andrews gathered in Mason's office.

Mrs. Bancroft said tearfully, "I can't ever tell you how much what you have done means to me, Mr. Mason."

Bancroft, pulling out a checkbook, said, "I can't tell you in words but I am going to try and write it on a check."

Mason said, "I am glad, Bancroft, that you had the nerve, the decision and the manhood to stand up and make the statement you did in open court. You will find now that life is a lot better and a lot more livable as far as you are concerned."

Mason came around the desk. "I am going to shake hands with you," he said. "It is a pleasure to shake hands with a real man."

The lawyer shook hands with Bancroft.

Rosena impulsively kissed the lawyer and then Phyllis Bancroft kissed him on the other cheek.

Mason, with lipstick on both cheeks, glanced with a smile at Della Street.

Della gently pursed her lips.

"We may as well make it unanimous," she said.

THE END